"You are *not* going to traipse down to the wharf alone at eleven o'clock at night."

A little thrill raced down Kacie's back. She couldn't help it. "He'll never talk if he sees you there."

"Who said he's going to see me?"

She waved her hand over Ryan's imposing form. "Little hard for someone like you to blend in."

"I have my ways."

"As long as you stay out of sight. I don't want you spoiling my meeting."

"How about saving your life?" He pushed back from the table and stepped around it to pull her chair out for her. "Is that okay with you?"

She nodded as silly schoolgirl butterflies took flight in her belly.

She'd have to watch herself with this man, in more ways than one. Because she couldn't let a sexy grin and a pair of strong arms deter her from exacting her revenge.

THE
WHARF

—

CAROL ERICSON

Recycling programs for this product may not exist in your area.

To my editor Allison, who gets it

ISBN-13: 978-0-373-69785-4

THE WHARF

This edition published by arrangement with Harlequin Books S.A.

For questions and comments about the quality of this book, please contact us at CustomerService@Harlequin.com.

Printed in U.S.A.

ABOUT THE AUTHOR

Carol Ericson lives with her husband and two sons in Southern California, home of state-of-the-art cosmetic surgery, wild freeway chases, palm trees bending in the Santa Ana winds and a million amazing stories. These stories, along with hordes of virile men and feisty women, clamor for release from Carol's head. It makes for some interesting headaches until she sets them free to fulfill their destinies and her readers' fantasies. To find out more about Carol, her books and her strange headaches, please visit her website, www.carolericson.com, "Where romance flirts with danger."

Books by Carol Ericson

CAST OF CHARACTERS

Ryan Brody—A small-town police chief, he agrees to help Kacie Manning research a book about his father, which unleashes a chain of events that he can't control any more than he can control his attraction to Kacie.

Kacie Manning—A true-crime writer who has an ax to grind with the Brody family, but her secrets are about to explode in her face, threatening her life and her tentative relationship with Ryan Brody.

Douglas Walker—This killer thought he had Kacie in the palm of his hand, but the book she wrote about him is less than flattering. Now he's out for revenge.

Duke Bannister—An ex-con who tries to warn Kacie and ends up with a target on his back.

Cookie Phelps—She was the last one to see Detective Joe Brody alive on the bridge, but she's not telling everything she knows about that fateful night.

Marie Giardano—The SFPD records clerk has always been a friend to the Brody brothers, but even that friendship can't protect her from people who think she knows too much.

Mrs. Rigoletto—The widow of Joseph Brody's partner may have dementia, but what secrets lie behind her vacant stare?

Layla French—The Phone Book Killer's first victim ties the past and the present together.

Russ Langford—Kacie's long-lost father may hold the key to the identity of the Phone Book Killer, or he may just be out for his own revenge.

Chapter One

The clanging of the halyards against the masts of the sailboats docked at the pier echoed across the water, sounding like a death-knell chorus.

"He wants revenge against you for tricking him, and he's gonna get it if you don't watch yourself."

Kacie Manning's back tingled with the warning, as if someone had already placed a target there. She peered at the man three feet away from her. His face was obscured by a baseball cap pulled low on his forehead and a bandana hiding his mouth and chin.

"Would you be willing to go to the police and tell them what you just told me? He can't make threats like that from prison."

The figure hugging the shadows hunched his shoulders. "I'm not getting on his bad side. The man's a straight-up psychopath. If the warden pays him a visit, Dan's gonna know who talked."

Kacie hugged herself, dipping her hands into the sleeves of her baggy sweater to ward off the chill of the night... and his words. "How's Dan going to get the word out on the street? The prison monitors his communication."

The man whistled between his teeth, and the bandana puffed out from his face. "I thought you knew Daniel Walker. You wrote a book about him, didn't you?"

"You know that, or we wouldn't be here."

"Then you should know what he's capable of, Kacie. He ain't just a psycho. He's a crafty psycho."

Goose bumps raced across her flesh, and she rubbed her arms. This ex-con obviously knew Daniel Walker well. Not everyone did—his own family sure hadn't. "Did he actually confess to the murders?"

"No way." He scratched at his chin beneath the bandana. "He's too smart for that. He still wants to keep on pretending. He started talking to me about karma one day before my parole. I didn't know what the hell he was talking about, but then he explained it's like revenge, comeuppance. And he told me you were gonna get yours."

"Why are you telling me this? Why are you warning me?"

"I dunno." He shuffled a step closer, careful to keep his face in the darkness. "You're a pretty little gal, Kacie. I saw you once or twice when you came to the big house to interview Walker."

She tried to swallow, but her dry throat wouldn't allow it.

He'd seen her at Walla Walla? Maybe Walker had sent *him* to take care of his business. She shuffled back a few steps. "That still doesn't explain why you'd risk Walker's anger to warn me."

"You remind me of my sister a little bit." His eyes glittered in the dark. "Besides, I ain't risking nothing. It's not like you're going to go running to Walker telling him someone from the state pen warned you about him, right?"

"Of course not."

A squeaking noise to her right made her grit her teeth. She jerked her head to the side and spotted a shopping cart rumbling around the corner, with a ramshackle man in rags steering it.

The parolee across from her swore and spit from beneath his bandana.

The homeless man trundled toward them, one wheel of his cart squealing and wobbling over the cement walkway.

Kacie held her breath as he drew next to them.

"Can you spare some change?" His hand was already protruding from the dirt-encrusted sleeve of his jacket.

Her informant had ducked back into the shadows, but his voice lashed out at the transient from the anonymity of the darkness. "Move it along, buddy."

The homeless man must've heard something in the other man's voice because he thrust his cart in front of him and picked up his ambling pace without a word or backward glance.

The transient had enough street smarts to recognize a dangerous man when he heard one. What was her problem? Could she even trust an ex-con wearing a bandana across his lower face?

She scooped in a breath of salty air. "Like I was saying, I have no reason to tell Walker anything."

"You sure he didn't charm the pants off you? Make you wet?" The man chuckled low in his throat.

Kacie clenched her jaw where a muscle jumped wildly. He was just trying to make her uncomfortable, push her buttons.

She snorted. "Did you read my book?"

"I don't read no books, but I heard about it. You tried and convicted the guy all over again and kicked him for good measure."

"Then you should know his smooth talk didn't work on me."

"You're a good actress, Kacie."

She flinched. She wished he'd stop using her name. They weren't friends. They weren't even acquaintances.

"Why do you say that?"

"'Cuz Walker thought he had you eating out of the palm of his hand during all those interviews you two did together."

"Oh well." She tossed her hair over her shoulder.

"That's why he was so pissed off. It's not just that you wrote a book that made him look bad. It's that he thought he had you."

"He thought wrong." And she'd done nothing in the interviews that would've made him think otherwise. She'd come into the project suspecting an innocent man had been convicted of murdering his wife and children. Several interviews later, she knew she was dealing with a sociopath, a *guilty* sociopath.

"Yeah, he had you all wrong." He adjusted his cap with a hand sporting a tattoo of a cross on the back. "That's why he wants to kill you."

The wind whistled in from across the bay and blew right through her. She huddled into her sweater further. "Thanks for the heads-up." She dug into her pocket for a hundred-dollar bill, creased it and held it out to him.

Stepping back, he sucked in a breath. "I ain't no snitch. I didn't tell you for money."

"I'm sorry. I didn't mean to offend you." She crumpled the bill in her fist and shoved it back in her pocket. "I appreciate the warning, that's all."

"Sure, sure. I told you. You remind me of my sister."

He pivoted, melting into the shadow of the building.

Kacie took one step away and cranked her head over her shoulder. "What were you in for?"

The voice came from the darkness like disembodied evil. "Killing my sister."

Kacie's hand flew to her mouth and she stumbled toward the weak light spilling from the ticket booth for the submarine. Her heart hammered so hard she wouldn't have been able to hear footsteps even if they were coming straight toward her.

This time she didn't care if she gave him the satisfaction of knowing he'd shocked her.... He had. She broke into a jog, heading for the lights at the more popular end of the wharf—not that teeming crowds met her here, either. Late on a Sunday night, Fisherman's Wharf wasn't exactly crackling with tourists and street performers. The fishermen had hauled in their catches many hours before and would be ready to go out in a few more. The hipsters and club hoppers were ducking in and out of bars in other areas of the city—other areas where the air didn't reek of fish and resound with the clanging of masts.

Her footsteps carried her past the darkened and shuttered restaurants, past the homeless people huddled on benches or in doorways. She kept glancing over her shoulder, half expecting to see the masked face of the sister-killing parolee. He'd probably just been trying to yank her chain. Was there anyone in prison who didn't lie?

If San Francisco were the type of city where you could hail a taxi on the street, she'd do it. No point in standing on a dark corner placing a call and waiting for one to show up.

Her legs moved faster. A few die-hard T-shirt shops still hoped for the odd tourist on a late-night souvenir run. The lights spilling from their windows tempered her pulse rate.

When she hit the street that led to her hotel, her breathing almost returned to normal.

A hotel near Fisherman's Wharf wouldn't have been her first choice, but Ryan Brody was staying there, so it was good enough for her.

He had at least two brothers living in the city, so she couldn't figure out why he didn't stay with one of them. Maybe there was a rift in the family.

Her lips stretched into a humorless smile. If that was the case, it couldn't happen to a better bunch.

Brody. The name filled her with unspeakable rage.

Kacie let out a pent-up breath as she hiked up the sidewalk to her hotel. A few more people, other than the transients who owned the night, crisscrossed the street and wandered into the shops still selling their wares.

Kacie greeted the bellhop as she stepped through the doors of the hotel. "Is the hotel pool still open?"

"It's open twenty-four hours, ma'am."

"Thanks."

When she got to her room, she fired up her laptop. She planned to find out the identity of her talkative ex-con. As the computer booted up, she shed her clothes and wriggled into a bikini. Then she grabbed the hotel-issued terry-cloth robe and threw it over the back of a chair.

She leaned over the laptop, her hands hovering above the keyboard. What was the murder of a sister called? Fratricide? Or was it something different for a sister?

She tapped the keyboard. He'd been imprisoned at Walla Walla, but that didn't necessarily mean he'd committed his crime in Washington.

She twisted her stiff neck from side to side and then shoved the computer away. She could do this the next morning before she met with Ryan Brody. Right now, she needed a little relaxation.

She slipped her arms into the robe and knotted the sash around her waist. Twisting her hair around her hand, she headed for the bathroom. Her toiletry bag hung on a hook on the back of the door, and she dug inside one of the pockets until her fingers tripped across a hair clasp.

She secured her hair, dropped her key card in her pocket and pulled her door securely closed behind her.

The vacant indoor pool beckoned. She shrugged out of

the robe and draped it over a chair. She jerked her head toward some splashing coming from the hot tub. Three teenage boys rose from the bubbling water in unison, steam floating off their bodies.

They better not be heading toward the pool. She sat on the edge and lowered herself into the lukewarm water. She kicked off the wall, and the water enveloped her as she sliced through it, her arms windmilling and her flutter kick just breaking the surface.

In, out, in, out. Her regulated breathing calmed her and cleared her brain of all the ugliness she dealt with on a daily basis—all the ugliness yet to come.

She finished her laps and, placing her hands flat on the deck, hoisted herself out of the pool.

One glance at the hot tub and a trail of water leading to the door told her the boys had left. She made a beeline for the sauna. She pulled one of the heavy doors open and poked her head inside where the dry heat blasted her. It was blissfully empty inside. She spread her towel out on one of the wooden benches and stretched out on her back, crossing her arms beneath her head.

She'd play it cool with Brody. She'd play it nice and civil—just like she had with Daniel Walker. Not that Ryan Brody, youngest police chief in the state of California, was a serial killer.

But his dad was.

She stretched out her legs and wiggled her toes. It felt great, but she couldn't take much more than ten minutes in the sauna.

A sound at the doors had her doing a half sit-up. She stared at the heavy wooden doors but nobody entered the sauna.

Good. Maybe someone had heard her in there. She rolled to her stomach, burying her face in her arms.

Sweat trickled down her back and dripped from her elbow. Sitting up, she dabbed the corner of her towel between her breasts.

She swung her feet to the floor and ladled a small amount of eucalyptus oil over the hot rocks. They sizzled and the fresh scent of eucalyptus soaked the room.

She took a few deep, cleansing breaths and then stood up and pushed at the door. It wouldn't budge.

She wiped her hands on her towel and grabbed one of the door handles with two hands and gave it a shove. Wedging her shoulder against the wood, she drove into one door and then the other. The doors stayed firmly in place and now her shoulder hurt.

What the hell? The bellhop had told her the pool area was open all night and the sign on the door had verified that. There was no way they'd be locking up now. And why would they lock the sauna from the outside?

She pushed at the doors again and heard a rattle against the wood.

"Hello? Is anyone out there? Can you open the doors?"

Only the hissing and dripping of the rocks answered her.

She scanned the walls of the sauna for a phone, an emergency shutoff or a call button and saw nothing but smooth, dry wood.

"Hey!" She pounded her fists against the doors. "I'm in here."

Sweat poured off her face and she mopped it with her towel. Trickles of it ran down her chest to her belly and more droplets crept down her spine.

Her breathing shortened and she parted her lips to drag in a long breath. The dry air filled her lungs.

She dumped another ladle of oil on the rocks and gulped in the rising steam.

Someone had to come in there shortly. If the pool was

open twenty-four hours, maybe the cleaning crew came in the middle of the night.

She tried one of the doors again, driving her shoulder against it. Again, she heard a rattling on the outside. Was there something blocking the door? A sauna wouldn't have a lock on the outside.

She planted her feet on the wood floor and flattened her palms against the double doors. She dug in and pushed with her entire weight. One of the doors moved past the other about a half an inch.

She pressed her eye to the crack, but the doors were too thick and there was very little space between them.

She put her lips to the space between the doors and screamed. "Help! I'm locked in the sauna."

The yelling weakened her, and her knees wobbled. She put a hand out for the bench and sank to its hot surface, which scorched the backs of her thighs. Everything was hot now.

She ran her tongue around her parched mouth and tipped her head back to peer at the ceiling. She eyed a square vent with mesh across it. Could she fit through that? Where did it lead?

She stood on the bench and reached for the vent, her fingertips skimming the mesh. She rolled up her towel and stood on top of it. She slammed the heels of her hands against the vent and then noticed the screws.

With nothing gained except sore palms, she lowered herself to the bench.

Her robe. She'd left her robe hanging over one of the chairs. Maybe someone would notice it from the gym that looked out onto the pool and come out to pick it up.

She pressed her face against the double doors again and screamed. "Help! I'm in the sauna."

She was going to meet her death in a hotel sauna. A

laugh bubbled to her lips. Her parents were going to have a helluva lawsuit.

She pressed her hands to her hot, moist face and her eyelids fluttered. How long had she been in there? Maybe she'd just pass out, and they'd find her in the morning.

She dropped to the bench before her knees could buckle under her. She'd try screaming again in a minute or two—when she got her breath back.

A voice! Had she imagined it?

She hopped up, adrenaline surging through her body. "Is someone there? I'm in the sauna."

Scratching and scraping noises echoed from outside the sauna and the doors wobbled. Then they flew open and cool air rushed into her wooden prison.

She heard a male voice, strong and angry. "What the hell happened?"

Her legs couldn't support her and she fell forward.

Her rescuer caught her in a pair of solid arms, and for a moment she melted against him. "Thank you. Oh my God, I was trapped in there."

"You're burning up. You need water." The man took a step back and tilted up her chin.

Her gaze met a pair of murky green eyes, which widened and grew lighter.

Her mouth dropped open, and her body jerked. She'd just fallen into the arms of the enemy.

Chapter Two

Ryan swallowed and then choked. "I'll be damned."

Kacie Manning's eyelids drooped and her body went limp again. He swept her up in his arms and carried her to a chaise longue. "Hold on. I'll be right back."

He dashed into the gym next door and grabbed his bottle of water from the floor next to the fly machine. By the time he'd returned, Kacie had opened her eyes, but they still hadn't lost their glassy look.

He held the bottle to her dry lips. "Drink this."

She parted her lips and he tipped the water into her mouth. She sputtered and coughed, then chugged half the bottle.

He poured some of the water into his cupped hand and splashed her face. She blinked a pair of impossibly long lashes and sniffled.

"Sorry, but you need to cool down."

"I—I'm okay." She reached for the bottle and downed the rest of the water.

"How long were you in there?"

"I have no idea. Was it locked from the outside? Why didn't it open?"

He held up a finger. "Hold on."

He grabbed the empty bottle, filled it up from the water

dispenser in the gym and swung by the sauna to pluck the pool net from the tiled floor.

He sat in the chair next to Kacie's chaise and handed her the bottle. "More."

While she wrapped her lips around the bottle, he held up the pool net by its long handle. "This was shoved across the doors."

"What?" She dropped the bottle onto the tile, where it spun, its mouth ending up pointing his way.

"I was working out in the gym. I just sat down on the fly machine and noticed the handle of the net wedged between the door handles of the sauna. I didn't know if it was a joke or what, but it looked dangerous."

"Someone shoved that across the handles while I was in there." She dabbed wet fingers across her forehead. "But it was no joke. I was getting weak and dehydrated."

"Was there anyone out here when you went into the sauna?" Her flushed red cheeks and bright eyes made her look younger than her picture.

"There were some teenage boys horsing around in the hot tub when I first came down, but they'd left by the time I hit the sauna."

"They could've come back."

Her eyes darkened to rich chocolate and her nostrils flared. "Maybe. I'm reporting it to the hotel."

"Of course."

It seemed ridiculous to introduce himself now after he'd held her half-naked body in his arms, but protocol demanded it if they were going to work together. He cleared his throat and thrust out his hand. "I suppose we should start from the top with a more formal introduction. I'm Ryan Brody. It's nice to finally meet you in person, Ms. Manning, even though the circumstances could've been better."

"Kacie Manning." She gripped his hand in a firm shake and then her face reddened even more as she glanced down at her wet bikini, plastered to her body and covering just the bare essentials.

Dropping his hand as if he had the cooties, she jerked upright and swung her legs from the chaise.

He hunched forward in his chair, ready to catch her in case she toppled over. "Whoa. You shouldn't be making any sudden moves. Do you want more water?"

"I want," she said, her gaze darting across the pool, "my robe."

"I don't think that's a good idea yet." He swirled his finger in the air. "You want to give your skin plenty of ventilation."

It sounded good, anyway. Truth was, he didn't want her covering up that beautiful body just yet. The small triangles covering her breasts and nestled between her legs left the rest of her curves on stunning display. The photo on her book cover of her in a blouse and jacket hadn't done her justice. She'd probably sell even more books if she posed in this bikini.

Good thing she couldn't read his male-chauvinist thoughts. His earnest look must've won out over his lustful one because she collapsed against the chaise longue, crossing her legs primly at the ankles.

"You're right." She pressed the back of her hand to her cheek. "But I think my body temperature is returning to normal."

At least someone's was.

He scooted his chair closer to her and leaned forward, brushing her wet hair aside and skimming his fingers across her forehead. "You're hot."

Her gaze slid to his face and she folded her arms across

her chest. "I think maybe I should get back to my room, get some clothes on and report this to the hotel."

"I'll help you." He scooted his chair back and held out his arm for support as she rose from the chaise.

She ignored him, but not for long. As she straightened up, she swayed to the side and clutched at his proffered arm.

He curled the other one around her bare waist. "Take it easy. Just lean on me."

She took a few shuffling steps and then dragged in a long breath. "I think I'm good now."

"I can carry you up to your room. It'll make your complaint to the hotel even better."

Her dark eyes flashed and he felt their heat. He'd gone too far.

He raised his hands, palms facing forward. "Just a thought."

She swept her robe from the back of a chair and folded it around her body. The entire pool deck seemed to drop a few degrees.

By the time she reached the door to the hallway, her steps were steady. She turned toward him. "What are you doing at the hotel? I wasn't expecting you until tomorrow."

"I left work early and decided to make the drive down tonight instead of in the morning. Don't feel compelled to move up our meeting time from lunch tomorrow just because I'm already here."

"Lunch still works for me." She shook her head and smiled. "Crazy way to meet."

"I'm just glad I decided to hit the gym for a late workout."

"Me too."

She checked out his shoulders and arms, visible in his

49ers muscle T, making him glad he'd just been pumping iron.

He ushered her into the elevator before him. "Floor?"

"Fourth."

He got off on the fourth floor with her, and she raised her eyebrows. "Are you on this floor, too?"

"One more up, but I'm not leaving you alone."

"I'm not going to faint, Brody."

"You never know. You were sweating buckets."

"That must've looked…attractive." She shoved her key card into the door and a row of green lights flashed.

"That looked scary. You lost a lot of fluids in that sauna."

She shoved her door open and then spun around, wedging her hands on either side of the doorjamb. "You can wait out here while I change. If you hear a big thump, you know I went down."

The door slammed in his face, and he jumped back. A little hostile, but he could understand why she wouldn't want a strange man lounging in her hotel room while she got dressed.

And they *were* strangers, despite their intimate beginnings on the pool deck.

When she'd first called him a few months before, he had recognized the name. Hell, he'd already read her book on Daniel Walker. Fascinating stuff—former college-football player, respected businessman, Pop Warner coach—went berserk and murdered his entire family.

When she'd proposed writing a book on his own family tragedy, it piqued his interest. Kacie Manning, like many others, believed in his father's innocence, and she had the resources, research skills and platform to prove it.

In the end, he'd had to run it by his brothers, especially Sean and Eric, the two oldest. They'd known Dad the best and had been affected by the dark cloud over the Brody name more than he and his younger brother, Judd, had been.

He'd braced himself for their opposition, but they surprised him by agreeing, or at least not objecting. They'd even uncovered a few pieces of evidence about the old case that Ryan planned to hand over to Kacie.

A loud thud resounded from Kacie's room, and he banged on her door. "You okay in there?"

The door eased open and she poked her head out. "I'm still upright, but my suitcase isn't—fell off the stand."

"Are you ready?" He nodded at the water bottle in her hand. "Keep hydrating."

"I'm so hydrated I'm ready to float away." She stepped out of her room, pulled her door shut and shoved her key card in her back pocket.

As he followed Kacie down the hallway, he scanned her fully clothed form. The addition of a faded pair of jeans and a baggy T-shirt did nothing to conceal her attractiveness. Damn. At the pool, he'd figured his male libido had just been reacting to the way she filled out that bikini.

But this new iteration of Kacie Manning heated his blood as much as the bikini-clad one. The soft denim of her jeans tightened in all the right places, accentuating her rounded derriere. She'd finger-combed her shoulder-length copper hair into tousled, damp waves that looked as if she'd just had a roll in the sheets.

He couldn't help it. Her appearance tweaked all his male parts. He had a hard time reconciling this lush body with the mind that had written that unflinching portrayal of a killer and sociopath.

Of course, if he ever admitted that thought to his brother's fiancée, Christina, she'd slap him upside the head.

Passing the elevator, she pointed down the hall. "Stairs."

He reached the door before her and held it open. "After you."

Walking closely behind her down the stairwell, he had a hard time concentrating on the steps and almost tripped on the last one.

"I thought I was the unsteady one." She pushed through the fire door and strode into the deserted lobby. Her flip-flops slapped against her feet as she marched to the front desk.

The hotel clerk put down his coffee and met her eyes across the counter. "Good evening. My name is Michael. Can I help you?"

Kacie flattened her palms on the shiny wood and hunched forward. "Well, Michael, someone locked me in the sauna over an hour ago."

The man's eyes bulged from their sockets. "The sauna doesn't lock from the outside."

Pushing the waves from her face, Kacie shook her head. "I don't mean locked. Someone used the handle of the pool net to wedge the doors closed."

"That's terrible! Are you okay? Do you need a doctor?"

"I'm fine…now." She jerked her thumb over her shoulder. "He was in the gym and noticed the net. He let me out."

"It's lucky you're both night owls. Did you see who did it?"

"No. There were some teenage boys in the hot tub earlier, but I don't have any proof that they did anything."

Ryan rested his arm on the counter. "Do you have a camera out there?"

"Sorry. We don't." He grabbed the receiver of his phone and barked into it. "Wesley, we have a situation in the lobby."

Kacie sighed and straightened up. "Then I don't know what you can do about it. The pool area and gym were empty when I went into the sauna. I heard a noise at the door about five minutes after I went in there. That must've been when the idiot decided to play his dangerous joke."

A security guard crossed the lobby, his rubber-soled shoes squeaking on the marble tiles. "What's the problem?"

"Miss…?" Michael raised his brows at Kacie.

"Manning, Kacie Manning."

His forehead furrowed. "Wesley, Ms. Manning was the victim of a rather dangerous practical joke. Someone wedged the sauna doors shut while she was in there."

Wesley tipped back his hat and scratched his forehead. "You don't say. That's a pretty stupid thing to do, especially at this time of night. Did you see anyone?"

"Just a few teens earlier, but they'd left by the time I went into the sauna."

"Yeah, I saw those boys. I had to kick them out of the business center tonight. They were dripping water all over the computers and accessing porn sites." Wesley cleared his throat. "Sorry, ma'am."

Kacie waved her hand. "Oh, I know all about pornographic sites and that teenage boys—and even grown men—are big fans of them."

Ryan slid her a sideways glance. Was that for his benefit? He'd better get his mind out of the bedroom and keep his eyes off her assets.

He stood tall and squared his shoulders. "If the boys were still wet, it sounds like they came straight from the pool. Where'd they go after you kicked them out of the business center?"

"I watched them get into the elevator, and I didn't see them again. I'm assuming they went back to their rooms, but they could've snuck back down to the pool."

Drawing her brows together, Kacie said, "I don't think

they had enough time if they were fooling around in the business center after they left the pool."

The security guard turned to Ryan. "Sir, did you see anyone in the gym?"

"Nope."

"The best I can do is talk to the boys if I see them again." He wagged his finger at Kacie. "You need to be more careful, young lady. Didn't your mama ever tell you to let someone know where you're going at all times?"

Kacie covered her twitching lips with her hand. "No, sir, but that's good advice."

Wesley tugged his pants over his significant belly and sauntered away.

"Sorry about that, Ms. Manning. Wesley's kind of old school."

"I didn't mind."

"We do want to make this up to you, however. I'll check with management, but I'm going to suggest we comp your stay with us, Ms. Manning." He bent his head over his keyboard and started tapping.

"Thanks, Michael." Kacie pointed at Ryan and mouthed the words *You too?*

He shook his head. He hadn't been the one sweating it out in the sauna.

Michael looked up from his task. "Oh, this is a coincidence."

"What is?" Kacie folded her hands on top of the counter.

"I left a message on your hotel phone earlier, probably when you were by the pool. I knew your name sounded familiar."

"Oh? What was the message? I didn't notice one on my phone."

"It's a package, actually. Some transient came in here with it, said a woman had dropped it out front. Your name was on it, and when I looked it up, I discovered you were a guest at the hotel."

"A package?" She shoved back from the counter and shrugged at Ryan. "I wasn't carrying anything except my purse when I walked back to the hotel tonight."

Michael rubbed his chin. "It had your name on it. I put it in the back. I'll get it."

"That's weird. I didn't bring any package with me."

"Maybe someone was supposed to deliver something to you and left it with a doorman or bellhop, and it got left outside. At least your name's on it, and the transient brought it in here."

"I hope it's not important. That's a pretty shabby way to treat something important."

Michael scurried from the back, balancing a lumpy, brown paper–wrapped package on his outstretched palms. He presented it to Kacie, her name scribbled in black felt pen across the outside. "Here you go, Ms. Manning. If there's anything we can do to make your stay more comfortable, please don't hesitate to ask."

"Thank you." She took the package from his hands and spun around. "I'm going to open this now."

She crossed the lobby and sank to the cushions of a love seat facing the door.

Ryan sat across from her and whipped out his knife. "Do you need something for the twine?"

"Yes, please." She held the package out to him, and he sliced the blade through the twine wrapped around the brown paper. It covered something soft and shapeless.

Placing the package in her lap, Kacie began unwrapping it. When she folded back the last piece of paper, she gasped and jerked back.

He lunged out of his chair, falling on his knees in front of her. "What is it? What's wrong?"

Holding the object with the paper, she turned it toward him. A rag doll with blond braids smiled at him with her stitched-on mouth.

His pulse slowed down. "A doll? Are you a collector?"

She shook the toy at him, and the braids flopped back and forth. "This isn't just some random doll."

His gaze tracked from the black button eyes of the doll to Kacie's own round eyes taking up half her face. "Obviously. What is it?"

"Daniel Walker's daughter was clutching this doll when he murdered her."

Chapter Three

The doll grinned at her with a mouth that resembled a slash of blood, calling up images of the original doll at the Walker murder scene. Kacie pressed two shaky fingers to the red yarn on the rag doll's face just to make sure it wasn't blood.

"Kacie, what does this mean?"

She raised her head, her eyes locking onto Ryan's as he put a steadying hand on her bouncing knee. The gesture had an immediate effect on her and she took a deep breath. She didn't have to face this alone right now. "Zoe Walker had a doll just like this one. When they found her body, she had one arm wrapped around her doll—this doll."

"I remember the doll from your book. This one's not yours, is it?" He flicked the paper with his fingers.

"No. This is the first time I've seen a doll like this since I saw the original. Someone sent this to me. That homeless guy didn't find a package outside the hotel. Someone probably paid him to deliver it to this hotel."

As a shiver rolled through her body, she pushed the doll from her lap, where it landed on the carpet still cradled in the brown paper.

"Wait." Ryan picked up two corners of the wrapping. "This might contain some evidence—fingerprints, hair, clothing fibers."

She shifted away from the doll as he placed the package next to her on the cushion and carefully folded the paper around the toy.

"Do you want to tell me why someone would want to send this particular doll to you?" He sat back on his heels as if he had all night to wait for an explanation.

She had no intention of making him wait that long. Despite her revulsion toward all things Brody, she couldn't deny the trust this man fostered in her bones.

He'd saved her from the sauna. His capable hands, square jaw and broad shoulders signaled stability and security. His green eyes reflected sincerity—when they weren't darkening to something more like lust, which happened anytime they wandered over her body.

The fears of the night, beginning with the fratricidal ex-con, flooded her senses, and her pulse rate galloped a mile a minute. She filled her lungs with a deep breath from her nose and expelled it through parted lips to ward off the rising panic and rushing adrenaline.

"Kacie, are you okay?" Ryan squeezed her knee.

"Fighting off an anxiety attack." She pointed to the ceiling. "I'll tell you all about this doll and who sent it from the comfort of my own room while holding a glass of wine in one hand."

"You got it." He sprang to his feet and held out his hand. "I'll help you up. One of my officers suffers from panic attacks, and she always gets a little dizzy."

She gripped his warm hand and struggled to her feet. "You have a cop working for you who has panic attacks?"

"Shh." He held his finger to his lips. "That's top secret."

"But you're her boss."

"That's right. She's a good cop. She told me about the attacks and it doesn't need to go any further—not that I think you'll go running to the Crestview City Council to report us."

Leaning against him, she tilted her head the other way to survey his face. "That's decent of you."

"I have totally selfish reasons. Like I said, she's a good cop and she makes the department and me look good."

She licked her lips. *Yeah, he probably likes the way that cop's backside looks in uniform.*

He kept his hand on her back and the package tucked under his other arm as he guided her toward the elevator. "I think we can skip the stairs this time."

As the doors closed, she stepped away from his warmth and wedged her shoulder against the cold mirror inside the car. "This has been quite a day—full of shocks and surprises."

She counted among those shocks and surprises her immediate attraction to Ryan Brody. The guy had it all in the looks department, including a killer bod, but she'd known that before their face-to-face meeting. She'd seen pictures of him and had even had her P.I. do a little surveillance on him in Crestview.

Brandy, the female P.I. she used, had gone a little overboard with some of the private pictures she'd gotten of Ryan with her long lens.

When Kacie had shuffled through the photos, including quite a few shirtless ones and even a grainy picture of Ryan coming out of his shower, she'd accused Brandy of forming an obsession over her subject.

Brandy, a lesbian in a committed relationship, had just winked.

Kacie's physical attraction to Ryan made up only part of the equation. The guy had rescued her from a scorching sauna. What girl wouldn't feel overwhelmed by that?

And then there was the way he had looked at her.

She glanced down at the body that for years had compelled her to sip diet sodas and munch raw veggies, while her two sisters and her mom could seemingly eat whatever they wanted and still maintain their svelte figures.

Ryan had eyed her as if he wanted to toss her over his shoulder and throw her down on the nearest bed or bend her over the nearest kitchen counter or take her against the wall—any wall.

She pressed her cheek against the cool glass of the mirrored elevator.

"Are you going to faint? Because I can carry you back to your room—piece of cake." He snapped his fingers.

The elevator doors whisked open and she stepped into the hallway, looking over her shoulder. "I'll save you the strain on your back."

His eyebrows jumped to his hairline and he cocked his head. "You're as light as a feather."

Great. How many weaknesses and insecurities could she reveal to him in the course of one night?

She invited him into her room and immediately abandoned the idea of the glass of wine. After the accusations against, and subsequent suicide of, his father, Ryan's mother had turned to drugs and alcohol. Kacie didn't want Ryan thinking she was a lush on top of all the other flaws she'd put on display that night.

Crouching in front of the little fridge, she asked, "Water? Something else?"

"If you're still having that wine, I'll have a beer—and I'll pay you back."

"I decided against the wine. Do you still want the beer? It's on the house."

"I still want the beer, and I'll still pay you for it."

She wrapped her fingers around a chilled bottle and held it up. "Is this okay?"

"That'll do." He reached over and took it from her and then twisted off the cap. "Now, tell me about that doll."

She snapped the lid on a diet soda and perched on the edge of the bed. "Like I told you before, the little Walker girl had the same doll. A strand of Walker's hair was found on the doll, and it was stuck on top of the blood smears. Walker's defense team and the prosecution went back and forth on this point. Walker's attorneys claimed that it wouldn't be unusual for a piece of their client's hair to be on his daughter's doll, and the prosecution argued that it got there *during* the murder."

"It was a significant piece of evidence."

"Yes."

"So, who sent you the doll and why?"

She pleated the bedspread with her fingers. "I think Walker sent it to me as a warning."

As Ryan sat next to her on the bed, she proceeded to tell him about her meeting with the ex-con and Walker's threats against her.

When she finished, he whistled between his teeth. "You're telling me earlier tonight you met with some ex-con who said he had info that Walker was after you?"

"Yep." She took a long pull from her can of soda, the bubbles tickling her nose.

"Damn, you live dangerously, woman."

"That's what I do. Do you think it was any picnic going to interview Walker at Walla Walla on visiting day?"

His gaze left her face and made a detour to her body before returning. "Umm, no. No picnic at all—for you."

It was a good thing her temperature was still slightly elevated because her cheeks warmed again at his taking inventory of her. She pursed her lips. Did he think she'd sashayed into the prison visiting room in a bikini?

"Did you catch this parolee's name?"

"No, but his initials are DB. That's how he signed his texts, anyway." She formed her fingers into a gun and pointed it at him. "That reminds me. He said he was in for murdering his sister. I was going to try to look him up."

"I can help you with that." He pushed off the bed and sauntered over to her laptop on the desk. "I can search for him on the law-enforcement database."

"That would be awesome. I was just going to try to search for fratricides in Washington that occurred about twenty years ago." She flipped up her laptop and turned it toward him.

"Why twenty years ago?"

"From what I could tell, the guy didn't look any older than fifty, so I figured maybe he served twenty or twenty-five years before his parole."

Ryan entered a website address and typed in a user-name and password at the log-in screen. "System's down. We'll check again tomorrow. I think you need to get to bed anyway."

Alone. Get to bed alone.

"I'm much better, thanks, but I'd appreciate it if you could stash that doll in your room." She drew up next to him, bumping his shoulder, and logged off the computer.

"No problem. I'll stuff her in my closet just so no one thinks I'm sleeping with dolls."

She jerked her head up and searched his face for a sign of the double entendre, but his clear green eyes, crinkling at the corners, showed only humor. All this talk of beds and sleeping had fired up her imagination again.

"Yeah, you wouldn't want that getting around your department." She backed away from him and swept his beer from the credenza. "Do you want to take this with you?"

"No, you can toss it." He grabbed the package with the doll wrapped inside and tucked it under his arm. "Do you want me to send this to the lab at the SFPD? Even though my brother's still on leave, I have connections there."

"I'll think about it, thanks."

He saluted and grasped the handle of the door, pulling it open. "Good night. We're still on for lunch tomorrow, right?"

"Yes, and now we have an advantage because we've already met. We can get right down to business."

"Yeah...business."

He stepped into the hallway and pulled the door closed, and Kacie let out a long breath.

That man had a way of making her feel like a siren or a femme fatale.

She fell across the bed, dangling her legs off the side. It didn't matter how Ryan Brody made her feel. She still had a job to do, and that meant proving his father's guilt beyond a reasonable doubt.

KACIE PICKED UP the receiver of the ringing phone once and dropped it back in its cradle, further burrowing into the pillows. She could sleep another few hours, but she'd been looking forward to this day for a few years. Never mind that Ryan had sort of spoiled the occasion by being even better looking in person than in his pictures and by saving her life and then saving her sanity by taking that doll away. Never mind all that.

It was game time.

An hour later she put the finishing touches on her makeup, dabbing the excess shine from her lips. She'd dressed in one of her prison outfits—a slim skirt that hit below the knee with a matching jacket—demure, plain, nothing to draw the unwelcome attention of the convicts at Walla Walla or Ryan Brody. He'd already seen her in next to nothing, but that was the night before. This was a whole new day.

She slipped her feet into a pair of low-heeled shoes and hitched her laptop case over one shoulder and her purse over the other. She even had the restaurant picked out for lunch, unless Ryan wanted to go somewhere else. She'd let him choose.

She always let them think they had the upper hand. It had worked with Daniel Walker up until the moment her book came out and he'd realized he'd been duped.

And apparently her trickery still burned a hole in his gut.

She made it to the hotel lobby fifteen minutes early and perched on the edge of the same love seat where she'd unwrapped that doll the night before.

She hunched her shoulders against the chill rippling up her back. What kind of man would send the same kind of doll his daughter had been hugging the moment he ended her life, as a warning? A sick one. But then, she'd only come to realize that about Walker later.

Like many others, she'd been swayed by Walker's good-looking, grief-stricken face…until she met the man.

She glanced up when the elevators across the lobby dinged open. Ryan strode through the doors and his head jerked in her direction like a heat-seeking missile.

She'd been waiting just five minutes, so he liked being early to meetings, too.

She still had the advantage of watching him approach. If everything that had happened the night before hadn't transpired, what would her first impressions of this man be?

Tall, good-looking, built, confident, maybe a little cocky. She sucked in her lower lip. This wasn't working. She couldn't forget the night before—his concern, his consideration, his blatant attraction to her.

"You're early." He offered a handshake. "I'm Ryan Brody, Ms. Manning. It's a pleasure to meet you."

She gripped his hand. "Are you trying to press the reset button? It won't work. I just tried it."

He squeezed her hand and wouldn't let go, as a smile spread across his face. "You're right. It doesn't work. I already know way too much about you."

At least he had the decency to keep his eyes on her face this time, but it didn't matter. Parts of her body tingled that didn't have any business tingling under her proper skirt and blouse.

He finally dropped her hand, and she smoothed her palms across the front of her linen skirt. "I don't know nearly enough about you, so I propose we get started. I made a reservation at Mezza Luna in North Beach, unless you have a preference for something else."

He spread his arms, and the cotton of his T-shirt tightened across his chest. "I'm a little underdressed. I thought since we were old friends, we'd be going more casual."

"You look fine." And *fine* had a whole other meaning for the way his jeans hugged his muscular thighs and tight backside.

"I can run up and throw on a sports coat, even though the summer weather is finally starting to peek through the fog."

"Mezza Luna isn't that formal, but it's a good place to conduct business. I like to feel like I'm dressing for work because this *is* my job."

"If you're sure they won't kick me out."

"I'm sure." She pointed to the front doors of the hotel. "I called ahead for a taxi. It should be here in about five minutes."

"I'm impressed you're so organized after the night you had."

She crossed her arms across her waist. "Speaking of which, where's the doll?"

"Stashed in the closet. Are you sure you don't want me to send it to the SFPD lab for analysis?"

"It's not against the law to send someone a doll, is it?"

"No, but if we can link it to Walker..."

"Oh, I know it's Walker. The ex-con told me Walker wanted to make my life a living hell, and the doll is his first shot."

"He's not going to have a second." He placed his hand on the small of her back and steered her toward the taxi, which had just pulled up.

Somehow she believed it when he said it.

He opened the door of the taxi for her and she slid across the seat, giving the restaurant's address to the driver.

It didn't take him long to get there, speeding through the streets, dodging cable cars and buses and maneuvering around pedestrians. The taxi squealed to a stop in front of the restaurant, and Kacie insisted on paying.

"Tax write-off for me."

Ryan took a detour to the men's room, leaving Kacie to confront the unfriendly hostess, who acted as if she were guarding the gates of Fort Knox.

Kacie dug in her heels. "Our reservation is for 12:45, and I requested a specific table. I don't think I should have to wait for that table."

The hostess pursed her lips and tapped her pencil on her reservation book. "We have a very important person coming later, and he always likes that table."

"Is there a problem with our reservation?" Ryan raised his brows at the hostess, his mouth turning up at one corner.

The hostess brightened up, flashing a set of white teeth

and pulling back her angular shoulders. "Not at all, sir. I'll seat you immediately."

Her slim hips swaying in front of them, she led them to their table.

If Ryan thought that woman had any intention of kicking him out of the restaurant for dressing too casually, he hadn't checked his reflection in the mirror.

Kacie pulled out her chair before Ryan could do it for her. He must have that effect on all women, not just her. She'd been silly to think his attention to her was anything more than his customary way of relating to women. Women loved him and he loved them back.

Good. She tugged on the lapels of her jacket. That made her job a lot easier.

Made lunch a lot easier, too. The hostess ensured that they had warm bread and cold water on their table in record time.

Kacie flicked open the menu, while munching on a piece of that bread drenched in olive oil.

"I've never been here before. Have you?" Ryan ran his finger down the sheet of daily specials.

"Once or twice. Everything's good."

"I think I'll go with the fettuccine with clam sauce."

"Excellent choice." She dabbed her fingers on the napkin in her lap. "Do you want to get down to business?"

"Sure, but can we finish last night's business first?"

Last night's business when she'd been ready to turn down her sheets for him at the crook of his little finger?

"We had unfinished business?"

"The security guard. Did he ever get back to you? Did he ever talk to those teenage boys?"

"I didn't hear from him, and there was a different clerk at the front desk this afternoon."

A waiter approached their table and took their order. When he left, Kacie pulled out her mini-recorder.

"I hope you don't mind if I tape our interview."

"Nope." He dug into the bread basket and dropped a piece on his plate. "You must have some fascinating recordings of Dan Walker."

"I do. A lot of times, it wasn't until I listened to the recording that I got to understand the man, as much as you can understand a sociopath. He's very distracting to talk to—he's such a good actor."

"And I'm not." He spread his arms. "What you see is what you get."

A total hunk with a protective streak a mile wide and a smile that could melt the insides of the snootiest, skinniest restaurant hostess in North Beach.

Kacie cleared her throat and set up her recording device. "That's good to know."

As she placed her finger on the record button, Ryan put his hand over hers like a caress. "Can I ask you a question before we get started?"

When he touched her like that, he could ask her anything. She flicked his hand off hers and pressed Record. "Go ahead."

He glanced down at the red light blinking on the recorder. "Why my father's story? Why are you interested in writing a book about a twenty-year-old cold case?"

"Because it *is* a cold case. Your father, an SFPD homicide detective, was suspected of being the Phone Book Killer, a serial killer he was investigating himself, but nobody ever proved it."

"A lot of people said he proved it when he jumped from the Golden Gate Bridge and the murders stopped."

"Damning evidence, but there are so many more who believe he was set up, and now all four of the sons he left behind are in some type of law enforcement. It's a great story." She shrugged her shoulders, stiff from her lies.

"You can count my two older brothers among those who believe in our father's innocence. They've recently stumbled across some new evidence and have agreed to give it to me to pass along to you."

Her water sloshed as she set down her glass. "Sean and Eric know I'm writing a book about the case?"

"Yeah. They're okay with it. I told them your angle is that someone set up Joseph Brody."

They wouldn't be okay with it if they knew her true purpose…and her true identity.

"Great." A smile stretched her lips. "And I'd love to see that new evidence. What do you remember about that time?"

"Not much. I was young and confused, and then I lost my dad, who was a larger-than-life figure for me." His green eyes darkened as he took a sip of water. "Do you still have both of your parents?"

"Y-yes."

He splayed his hands on the white tablecloth in front of him. "It's hard to explain the loss of a parent, especially at a young age. You can't begin to understand the hole it leaves."

Oh, but she could.

"You're right."

"And then I lost my mom." He studied his fingernails. "She turned to prescription drugs and alcohol, and Sean had to take over the parenting duties."

"Your mom passed away." She knew the whole painful Brody story.

"Not until I was an adult, but it was still tough. So many wasted years."

Their food arrived, and Kacie turned off the recorder.

Ryan's soulful eyes and sensitive mouth were going to make this a lot harder than she'd anticipated.

The smell of garlic and fresh clams wafted from Ryan's plate, putting her chopped salad to shame. She dug into her rabbit food as he twirled his fork into his creamy pasta.

They ate in silence for a few minutes before he pointed his fork at her salad. "Is that all you're having?"

"It's a big salad."

"It's a salad." He held his fork out to her, tightly wrapped in fettuccine, the savory steam curling beneath her nose. "Try some of this."

She tapped her plate. "Put it here."

"Then you'll have to twirl it up again. Here." He hunched forward, the fork centimeters from her lips.

She opened her mouth and he placed the fork against her tongue. She sealed her lips around the tines and sucked the pasta into her mouth as he drew the fork out with a flourish.

Tingles raced up her inner thighs and circled her belly. She grabbed her napkin and pressed it against the lower half of her face while she chewed. This craziness had to stop.

"Good, huh?" He grinned, but his heavily lidded eyes looked more seductive than smiley.

"Very good." She dropped the napkin from her still-warm face. "Now I will return to my regularly scheduled salad."

"Just let me know if you want another…taste."

She waved down the waiter. "More iced tea, please."

She had to find some way to stay cool. Did all this sex appeal come naturally to Ryan Brody, or was he cranking up the charm for some ulterior motive? She'd already told him she planned to focus the book on proving his father's innocence. He didn't have to butter her up.

Her gaze dropped to his strong hands as he ripped a roll in two and smeared a pat of butter across one half. Although she wouldn't mind if he buttered her up, down and sideways.

She'd *never* felt this way about a story resource before.

Holding up the roll, he asked, "Do you want the other half?"

"No, thanks." She pushed her plate away, dabbed water droplets from the tablecloth with her napkin and repositioned her recorder on the table.

"Whenever you're ready."

He polished off the rest of his meal, including the rest of her roll, and then perused the dessert menu. "Do you want to share a dessert?"

"I'm good."

He ordered a coffee instead and leaned back in his chair as he stirred in a swirl of cream. "Fire away. Ask me anything you want about my father's case. If I don't know the answer, I'll ask my older brothers."

Kacie flipped open her notebook, which contained sheets of printed-out questions. She dived in.

"The Phone Book Killer case was unusual from the get-go, wasn't it? After the first two victims, the killer started communicating with your father, one of the detectives on the case, claiming he was selecting his victims out of the phone book."

"That's right. Serial killers have been known to contact the police to brag and taunt, and the Phone Book Killer singled out my dad. Of course, that's one of the aspects of the case that caused some doubt about my father. Why him?"

"Good question." She drummed her fingers against the tablecloth. "Then he kidnapped your brother. Was that some kind of warning?"

"According to Sean, that's what my father thought. It

was the killer's message that he could get to any member of my family."

"But your brother wasn't harmed, which became another oddity of the case."

Ryan raised his shoulders and let them drop. "People say Joey Brody staged the kidnapping to divert suspicion from himself."

"Then the evidence from your father started to pile up— missing days from work, plaster found in the trunk of his car, the same type of plaster used in casts, which the Phone Book Killer was wearing to disarm his victims."

"Too pat. Too easy." He massaged the back of his neck. "In hindsight, it smells like a setup."

As she reeled off the elements of the case against Joey Brody, Ryan had an answer for every one of them. He had emphasized that his older brothers believed without a doubt in their father's innocence, and Ryan's hot defense of Joey Brody put him firmly in that camp.

Of course they were all in that camp. Admitting your father had blood on his hands had to be hard.

After another hour of question and answer, where they saw the restaurant clear out and received several visits from their waiter with more coffee and iced tea in hand, Kacie clicked off the recorder.

"I really appreciate your openness. It can't be easy. Y-your dad sounds like he was a great cop."

And Daniel Walker had been a great football player.

He shrugged. "Life is full of trials and tribulations. How about you? You look like you've had it pretty easy—smart, attractive, successful."

Straightening her shoulders, she folded her hands on top of the notebook. "I've been lucky. I have a wonderful family. Great parents, two older sisters."

"I hope you appreciate that."

Anxious to hide the emotion that had overcome her, she swiped her recorder from the table and ducked down to stuff it into her bag. "Oh, I do, but you're right." She popped back up with her phone and wallet in hand. "We all have our…disappointments in life."

A loud voice carried across the mostly empty restaurant. "Kacie Manning, right?"

She jerked her head up and zeroed in on a pudgy man with a black goatee making his way toward their table. "Do I know you?"

He stuck out his hand. "I'm Ray Lopez. I'm a reporter with a local TV show."

Great. That's all I need.

"Good to meet you, Ray." She gestured toward Ryan. "This is Ryan Brody. Chief Brody."

"Oh, hey. No introductions necessary. I know who Chief Brody is. I'm like this—" he held up two fingers pressed together "—with Sean and Eric. Eric's fiancée, Christina, and I go way back."

Ryan shook Lopez's hand, sizing him up with one glance. "Sure, I know who you are."

Kacie's gaze bounced from Lopez to Ryan. Sounded as if Ryan wished he didn't know Lopez.

"I'm a big fan of yours, Kacie. Is it true you're doing a book on Joey Brody?"

"You know, I'd rather not discuss that." She swirled the ice in her water glass and took a sip.

"Say no more." Lopez raised his hands. "It's just that I've been trying to get exclusives for years with the Brodys. Guess I'm the wrong sex or something."

Ryan tossed his napkin onto the table. "Excuse me?"

"Just a little joke, Brody. I'd rather work with Kacie Manning than with me, too." He winked and sauntered back to the hostess stand.

"What a jerk." Kacie rolled her eyes.

"He's been kind of a local fixture here the past few years."

"Does he really know your brothers?"

"Yeah, but Sean just tolerates him and Eric can't stand him." Ryan made a move for the check, which had been perched on the edge of their table for an hour. "Let me get this."

She beat him to it, snatching it up and pressing it to her chest. "Tax write-off, remember?"

As she snapped her plastic down on the tray, Ryan tapped her phone on the table. "You have a couple of messages."

"I heard them come through earlier." She picked up the phone. "Didn't want to disturb our flow."

"Yeah, we do have a flow, don't we?"

The hostess with the mostest had extricated herself from Lopez, who'd since left the restaurant. She parked herself next to Ryan's chair, batting her fake eyelashes. "Is there anything else we can do for you today?"

"No, thanks. Sorry we took up this table all afternoon."

"No problem." She waved her perfectly manicured nails. "I could see you were hard at work over here. If you like to play as hard as you work, a friend of mine is having a party tonight at a private club. I could get you in as my…guest."

Kacie clenched her teeth as she tapped her phone to view her messages. He could do whatever he wanted while he was here, including partying with pretty people, as long as he made himself available to her for their interviews and a few field trips.

But she didn't even hear his response as she read over her second message. The blood drained from her face and her head felt like a balloon ready to float away.

"Kacie?"

She glanced up from the display to meet Ryan's eyes, wide and questioning.

"Are you okay?"

The hostess backed up from the table. "I'll let you two finish your business."

Kacie dragged in a breath and released it through dry lips. "It's my contact from last night. He wants to meet again tonight."

"The ex-con?" He snapped his fingers for the phone. "No way."

She raised her brows. When had she appointed him her master scheduler? She handed him the phone anyway, realizing she'd have a hard time saying no to this man.

He peered at the display and read it aloud. "'Meet me same place as last night, same time. More info. DB.'"

He handed the phone back to her. "You recognize that number?"

"It's the same one he used before and the same initials." She pressed her damp palms against her napkin, still crumpled in her lap. "Maybe he knows about that doll. Maybe he saw who gave it to the homeless guy."

"Maybe you should ignore him."

"I can't. He's warning me about Walker."

"Or he's doing Walker's bidding. You ever think of that?"

"Yes. I'm not stupid."

"Oh, I know that, but you're not thinking clearly right now. You are *not* going to traipse down to the wharf alone at eleven o'clock at night."

"I have to go. He might have important information about Walker's next move against me, maybe something I can give to the police this time."

Ryan held up his hands. "You weren't listening. I said you weren't going there *alone*."

A little thrill raced down her back. She couldn't help it. "He'll never talk if he sees you there."

"Who said he's going to see me?"

She waved her hand to indicate his imposing form. "Little hard for someone like you to blend in."

"I have my ways."

She added a tip to the bill and scribbled her signature. As she tucked the receipt in the side pocket of her purse, she said, "As long as you stay out of sight. I don't want you spoiling my meeting."

"How about saving your life?" He pushed back from the table and stepped around it to pull her chair out for her. "Is that okay with you?"

She nodded as silly schoolgirl butterflies took flight in her belly.

This was exactly the effect Daniel Walker wanted to have on her—wrap her around his little finger, tell her sweet little lies.

What could Ryan Brody's motive possibly be? To make sure she wrote a favorable book about his father? She'd already told him she planned to do so. Did he doubt her?

She'd have to watch herself with this man, in more ways than one. Because she couldn't let a sexy grin and a pair of strong arms deter her from exacting her revenge on his father.

Her mom deserved justice.

Chapter Four

Ryan slung the towel over his shoulder, his gaze riveted on the pool area where three teenagers roughhoused in the water. They had to be the same ones from the night before.

He pushed through the glass door separating the weight room and the swimming area, and the humidity of the pool deck seeped into his flesh. The soles of his running shoes squished the wet tiles as he crossed to the edge of the pool. He squatted beside it and called out, "Hey."

Three faces turned toward him, a sullen look already forming around the mouth of one of them.

He was the one who answered. "Yeah?"

"Were you guys in here last night? In the hot tub?"

The three of them exchanged quick glances, and another teen spoke up, an earnest look on his face. "Yes, sir. We were in the hot tub late last night."

"Did you happen to see a woman out here?"

"Yeah, she went into the pool."

"She was smokin' hot for a cougar." The first boy to have spoken up stuck his tongue out of his mouth and flicked it up and down.

Ryan's hands, resting on his knees, curled into fists.

"Shut up, man." The Boy Scout punched his friend in the shoulder, then turned his attention back to Ryan. "Why are you asking? Did something happen?"

Flexing his fingers, Ryan dropped one knee to the deck. "Someone played a trick on her in the sauna."

The sullen one lost the attitude and the smirk and said, "She was still in the pool when we left."

The other two teens nodded in agreement. "She was swimming laps when we bolted."

"Did you see anyone else out here? In the gym?" Ryan pushed to his feet.

"No, sir."

"All right. Thanks." Ryan exited the pool area, mopping his face with the towel.

He believed them. According to the security guard, those boys were probably messing around in the business center at the time Kacie was in the sauna. Besides, would they play a trick like that on a smokin'-hot cougar?

They got half of that right. Kacie was smokin' hot, but she was no cougar—at least not for him.

He filled up his water bottle from the gym's dispenser and then tossed his towel in the bin. She'd shot him down when he asked her to join him for dinner that night, but they planned to get together before her meeting with DB to give him another crack at finding the guy in the law-enforcement database.

As far as he could tell, Kacie had spent the afternoon holed up in her hotel room—working, she said. He smacked the elevator button with the flat of his palm. That woman ran hot, very hot, and cold.

Women. He sure loved 'em, but he couldn't even pretend to understand 'em.

He'd spent his afternoon dropping that doll off at the local precinct, touching base with his brother's fellow officers and then tracking down his younger brother.

He knew Judd was going to be out of town again, but he'd managed to catch him for about an hour before he headed to the airport, this time to work for the Saudi royal family. His P.I. brother had been getting higher-end gigs lately, a step up from spying on errant spouses.

Ryan shook his head as he slipped his key card into his door. He'd barely recognized Judd with his suit sleeves covering his tattooed arms, his long hair slicked back.

Once again, Judd had offered up his apartment to Ryan, but Ryan had passed. Judd was careless with his business and his women. Ryan didn't want any surprises in the form of irate females dropping in—either ones Judd had spied on for their husbands or ones he'd loved and left.

That was the excuse he had given Judd, anyway. If he took his brother up on his offer, he'd have to check out of this hotel. And Kacie Manning was in this hotel, one floor below him. He wasn't going anywhere.

He showered, changed and ate a burger at the restaurant in the lobby. Then he showed up at Kacie's door, five minutes early.

She'd stacked the remnants of her own room-service meal on the credenza. Papers and notebooks littered the desk around her laptop. She'd swapped her business attire for a pair of black jeans and a dark green top that accented the copper highlights in her hair and an expanse of soft, creamy skin above the neckline.

Wedging her fist on one curvy hip, she tapped the toes of her bare foot. "You're early—again."

"Am I?" Had he betrayed his eagerness to see her?

"I was just going to clean up." She flicked her fingers toward the abandoned dishes.

"Let me." He hoisted the tray and carried it toward the door.

She scooted around him to pull the door open and then leaned against it while he pushed the tray against the wall in the hallway.

He rose, dusting his hands together. "I ran into those teenagers at the pool today."

"Really?" She let the door slam. "Did they fess up to anything?"

"Just that they thought you were smokin' hot." He would leave out the cougar part.

Color rushed into her cheeks, and she snorted. "Must've been all that steam from the hot tub obscuring their vision. So, they didn't see anyone else out there?"

"No." He tilted his head and hitched his thumbs in his pockets. Was she fishing for a compliment or did she really not understand the impact of that body on a red-blooded American male?

She ducked her head and fussed with the laptop, her hair creating a veil over her face.

Nope. She didn't get it. Self-confident about everything except her looks. He knew the type.

"I couldn't get back to that system you were using."

"I'll find it." He sidled next to her at the desk by the window and brushed her arm with his fingers as he reached for the keyboard.

Standing shoulder to shoulder with her, he felt her body quiver. Must be the excitement of discovering the identity of her contact. Couldn't have been because of their close proximity, since she'd been shoving him away from her with both hands ever since he'd carried her bikini-clad body from the sauna.

He pointed to her screen background, a middle-aged couple with a spaniel between them. "Your parents?"

"And their faithful dog. They've had him for fifteen years."

He studied the pair, a sleek blonde with straight chin-length hair and a balding man who looked fit for his age. Kacie must have taken after her dad because she didn't resemble her mom at all.

He entered a URL and typed in his username, pass-word and number from his token. The system whirred to life and he let out a breath. "It's up."

Kacie stepped away from him and planted a chair be-tween them. "Have a seat. I'll give you what I know."

He settled on the edge of the chair, his hands hovering above the computer as he waited for it to connect. When the search bar appeared, he turned his head to look at her. "Date of incarceration?"

"Can you enter a range of dates?" She leaned over him and her fragrant hair tickled his cheek.

He swallowed. "Yeah."

"Maybe twenty or twenty-five years ago."

He typed in the date range. "Location?"

"Let's go with Washington State." She jabbed her fin-ger at the display, and the side of her breast skimmed his upper arm. She pulled back.

He got rock hard. He squeezed his eyes shut and grit-ted his teeth. "Washington. Crime?"

"Murder."

He entered the man's heinous crime, but even that couldn't tame the heat surging through his body. He'd need a cold shower for that.

"I can't exactly enter his initials, but I can enter *B* fol-lowed by an asterisk and that should give us everyone with a last name starting with that letter—unless he's lying to you."

"An ex-con lying? Say it ain't so." She knelt down be-side his chair.

"Then this is it." He entered the initials in the name fields and clicked the search button.

A little hourglass blinked in the center of the display.

"Uh-oh. This could take a while."

"We have time." She rose from her seated position and

tapped at the clock in the lower right corner of the screen. Then she settled back on the floor. "Did you have a good afternoon?"

Leaning back in the chair, he stretched his legs out to the side. "I took that doll to the SFPD."

"You didn't have to do that. There's no crime."

"Doesn't matter. They know me there from my brother Sean, and besides, it's professional courtesy."

"Did you give them any details?"

"They didn't ask, and I didn't tell."

"Well, thank you." She folded her hands in her lap. "Did you get a chance to visit some old haunts in the city?"

"I dropped in on my brother."

"I thought he was on extended leave."

"My other brother—Judd."

"He's the youngest, right?"

"Youngest and wildest."

"He's a P.I."

That wasn't really a question. She seemed to know his family history as well as he did. "Yep."

"Why didn't you just stay with him?"

"He was on his way out of town, too. He's been doing some bodyguarding, and this time I think he's guarding a suitcase full of jewels instead of a person." Ryan's gaze dropped to the top of her head. Besides, all the excitement he needed was right here at this hotel in Fisherman's Wharf.

"Wow, I bet he has some stories to tell."

"If he does, he keeps them to himself." He jiggled the mouse to wake up the display. "Just last month he was working as a bodyguard for some pop princess on tour in Hawaii."

She snapped her fingers. "Oh, oh, I know who that

is, but her name escapes me now. Aren't you just a little bit envious?"

Right now, working with Kacie and enjoying the way her quick mind picked up on his next thought and their easy back-and-forth banter, he didn't envy anyone. "Naw. That's Judd's thing. He's kind of rootless. I like my small town."

"Of course, you did have an opportunity tonight to party with that attractive hostess." She threw up her hands. "Don't let me get in your way of a good time. If you want to check it out after we meet my informant tonight, go for it."

He drew in his eyebrows. Was she trying to push him into that hostess's arms? "Ah, not interested."

"Not a party kind of guy?"

He would prefer a party of two in that king-size bed across the room. Leveling a gaze at her, he said in almost an undertone, "I like certain kinds of parties."

She jumped to her feet and brushed off the seat of her snug jeans as she wandered to the window.

His voice must've betrayed his meaning, and it sure did fluster her. Either she wanted nothing to do with him, or he was growing on her.

"If you change your mind, I'm sure she'd welcome you with open arms."

The beep of the computer saved him from trying to analyze her obsession with sending him away with some other woman.

He hunched forward and scrolled through the entries. "There are quite a few here, but it won't be an impossible task to comb through them."

"Too bad we can't split them up."

"We can't." He rose from his chair and dragged the other one next to his and patted the seat. "So you might as well sit down next to me."

She moved the chair a few inches away from his and

sat on one corner, ready to take flight if necessary. "Okay, what do you do, just click on the entry?"

"That's it."

They spent the next fifteen minutes selecting the cons, and Kacie's shoulders began to get sore from holding them stiffly so she wouldn't accidentally brush against Ryan again.

When she'd accidentally mushed her breast against his biceps, she had nearly melted into a puddle. Of course, her chest had done a bunch of mushing against his when he'd carried her out of the sauna, and she'd been wearing a lot less then, but she'd been half out of it and hadn't yet formed this powerful attraction to him.

She rubbed the back of her neck as Ryan clicked on another possible suspect.

He swung his head toward her. "Are you tired?"

"My neck and shoulders are tight. I already put in a few hours of computer time this afternoon."

"Why don't you go stretch out on the bed? If anything looks promising, I'll call you over."

Her gaze darted to the bed and back to the computer. What would be worse, lying on a bed in the same room as Ryan or continuing to sit inches away from his hard body, inhaling his fresh, masculine scent?

She pushed back from the desk so fast her chair tipped back.

"Whoa." Ryan caught it and righted it.

She scurried to the bed, dragged the pillows from beneath the bedspread and punched them into position. Then she hopped onto the bed, her head sinking against the pile of pillows.

"Let me know if you find anything, and help yourself to the mini-bar."

He hunched over the laptop and continued tapping and clicking.

Good move. Her head began clearing once she was out of the Ryan realm. Without all his manliness parked next to her and invading her senses, her muscles relaxed and her breathing deepened. The sounds from the computer became hypnotic and she closed her eyes.

Rough fingertips dabbled against her cheek and she burrowed into the pillows, a smile curving her lips.

"Kacie?"

"Mmm." Warmth spread through her body and she felt safe, like the first time her foster parents brought her home.

She rolled to her side and flung out her arm. Her hand hit an immovable object, and she peeled open one eye.

Perching on the edge of the bed, Ryan smiled at her. "You dozed off."

She opened her other eye, noticed her hand resting against his thigh and snatched it back. She grabbed a pillow and hugged it to her body, bringing her knees to her chest.

"Was I out long?" Had she been snoring? Drooling? She wiped the back of her hand across her dry mouth.

"About an hour."

"Sorry." Why wouldn't he remove himself from the bed?

"No worries. You looked so peaceful over here I didn't want to disturb you."

She rubbed her eyes and scooched up to a sitting position, still clutching the pillow to her chest. "Did you find anything?"

"I did, just now." He jerked his thumb over his shoulder.

"You found DB?" Her fingertips buzzed and she dropped the pillow to her lap. She would've swung her legs off the bed, but Ryan's six-foot-something frame of solid muscle blocked her way.

He must've read the trapped-animal look in her eyes

because he eased off the bed and took a step back. "It looks like DB is Duke Bannister. He was convicted of first-degree murder and sent to the big house for twenty-five to life. Served twenty-two of those years and then got paroled last year."

Tossing the pillow to the side, she scrambled from the bed. "Who'd he kill?"

"His sister."

She tripped and he caught her around the waist. "Careful."

"Bannister told me I reminded him of his sister."

"Even more reason for me to come with you tonight." Ryan gave her hip a pat before releasing her.

Taking his vacated place in front of the computer, she dragged the chair forward and studied the screen. "Now that I know who he is, I can dig around his background and see if I can find out whether or not he's working for Walker."

"You may be able to find that out tonight."

"How?" She pushed her bedhead hair from her face. "He's not about to tell me if I ask him."

"You won't have to ask him. If he attacks you, you'll have your answer."

She hunched her shoulders. "That's not going to happen."

"Really? The dude killed his own sister."

"Okay, maybe you're right, but you're my muscle tonight." She bit her lip and busied herself printing out Bannister's page, second-guessing her plan to meet with Ryan in person. She'd have been better off conducting an interview with him over the phone or even over the computer. The man's presence was scrambling her thoughts and overloading her senses.

"We have about forty minutes. I'm going to get ready. Can we meet in the lobby in a half an hour?"

"Sure."

She strode to the door and opened it wide, watching him as he moved from the room into the hallway. "Thanks for doing all the work while I snoozed."

"No problem. It looked like you needed the rest."

She pulled the door closed and banged her forehead against it. She needed to wrap up this interview process and get down to the business of proving Joseph Brody's guilt beyond a shadow of a doubt.

She brushed her teeth, finger-combed her hair and stuffed her feet into a pair of canvas shoes. They'd do if she had to take off in a sprint.

Ryan had beaten her to the punch again, greeting her with a big smile in the lobby ten minutes early.

"Are you always early?" She threw her sweater over her shoulders, letting it hang.

"Are you?"

"Pretty much."

"Me too."

Drawing her small purse across her body, she asked, "How is this going to work?"

"Tell me where you met him last time. You start out first and I'll follow you, slinking along in the shadows. I won't be far behind you at any given time, but you won't see me and neither will Bannister."

"Should I use a code word or something if I get into trouble?"

"If you want to play spy games, go for it. Otherwise, a good old-fashioned scream will work."

"I mean—" she stepped through the front door of the hotel and nodded at the doorman "—if I start feeling nervous and I just want you to be primed and ready."

"I'm always primed and ready."

He winked at her and she rolled her eyes, but she could believe it with that body. "You know what I mean."

"I do. How about 'sauna'? It's where we first met, where I rescued you from danger the first time."

"The first time?" She raised her eyebrows. "Do you think there will be a second?"

"There could be tonight—that's the point."

"Okay, 'sauna' it is." She gave him the location of her first meeting with Bannister and set out ahead of him, her footsteps jaunty and her head held high.

The usual transients went about their usual business, but this time she eyed each one, wondering if he could have been the one who delivered the doll to the hotel.

The moist air off the bay caressed her face and worked through the waves of her hair. Even though she'd left the city as a child for Seattle with her new family, the smells and feel of San Francisco had never left her—and never would.

She cranked her head over her shoulder once, but couldn't see one trace of Ryan. He was probably taking a different route to stake out a good location, and with his dark clothing and 49ers cap pulled low on his face, he'd blend right into the scenery of the wharf.

Knots formed in her belly as she waited to cross the street before hitting the walkway along the wharf. Most of the restaurants were shutting down for the night or trying to, and all of the street performers had rolled up their props and gadgets from the sidewalk. Tourists still crisscrossed the streets, weaving in and out of the shops still open for business. The homeless population, the silent army of the night, shuffled from doorway to bench to bus stop, searching for a place to park their possessions.

She strode through the crosswalk and turned left toward

the less-populated area of the wharf, its tourist attractions long closed for the day. She spotted the low-slung building where she'd met Duke Bannister—assuming that was his actual name—the night before and dragged in a long breath.

Her gaze scanned the vacant side of the building. The last time he'd come from around the corner of that building. Easier for a surprise attack?

Tensing her muscles, she lightly clenched her hands at her sides. If Bannister got to her before Ryan got to him, she planned to do a little damage of her own first.

She slowed her steps and cleared her throat. "DB?"

If she used his real name, she might spook him. And she definitely wanted to hear what he had to say.

She froze. Had she heard a cough?

"DB?" She reached the building and trailed her hand along the damp metal, stopping at the corner.

"I-it's Kacie."

A soft sigh floated from around the corner of the building. Was he playing some kind of game with her?

"Are you there?" If Bannister was lurking around the corner in a suspicious manner, Ryan would notice that. Wouldn't he?

She held her breath and gripped the edge of the building. She leaned forward, turning her head to the side. A man sat on a bench facing the water, a hat perched on his head, one arm resting across the back of the bench.

"DB, it's Kacie." She crept forward, the soft soles of her shoes a whisper on the pavement.

Her jaw ached with tension, and her little sips of air had her lungs burning. She couldn't see his other hand, which could've been resting in his lap. Holding a weapon?

Her first swallow became a lump in her throat and she tried again. She approached DB from the back and laid a hand on his denim-clad shoulder.

Her fingertips met moisture. She snatched her hand back and peered at her fingers in the dim yellow light spilling from a bulb on the outside of the building.

The smell of blood invaded her nostrils—heavy, metallic. Rubbing her sticky fingers together, she circled the bench and dropped to her knees in front of DB.

Blood soaked the bandana around his neck as it gurgled from a gash across his throat.

As Kacie screamed "sauna," one thought pummeled her brain.

Duke Bannister's sister had finally gotten her justice.

Chapter Five

Ryan jumped from behind the barrels on the wharf and sprinted toward Kacie, her howl echoing in the night.

He pulled his gun from his pocket and charged toward the figure reposing on the bench, ready to do him physical harm if he had one finger on Kacie.

No need.

Kacie had fallen onto her backside, her hands spread before her.

Bannister's head lolled back, as if he were taking in the night sky, his denim shirtfront and blue bandana loosely tied around his neck soaked with blood. Someone had slit his throat from ear to ear, creating a grisly second smile.

Ryan dropped to the ground and pulled Kacie away from the dead man. Bannister's blood smudged her splayed hands, and without their support, she tilted to the side, in danger of falling over.

He wrapped an arm around her shoulders and pulled her close against his body. "Shh. Don't worry. I'm right here beside you."

She sobbed against his arm. "The blood, the blood."

Ryan placed his firearm back in his pocket and exchanged it for a cell phone. He called 911, then hooked his arms beneath Kacie's to bring her to her feet since she seemed incapable of movement.

"Hey, what happened, man? Is the lady okay?"

Ryan glanced over his shoulder to see a transient hunched over his shopping cart. "She's okay, but this guy is dead. Did you see anything? See anyone hanging around here?"

"Nope." The guy took off faster than he'd probably ever moved since he'd been on the streets.

Carrying Kacie toward a chain-link fence across from the bench, he whispered soothing words against her soft earlobe. "It's okay. I have you."

Her eyes grew wide and she clutched his T-shirt with both hands, forgetting they were stained with Bannister's blood. "What if he's still here? What if Walker is still here?"

He wrapped his arms around her trembling body and stroked her hair. "Walker's not here. He's locked up, remember? Nobody's going to hurt you."

She sniffled and burrowed against his chest.

His arms tightened around her trembling frame, and she molded against his body, melting into him. He could stand there all night holding her if it weren't for the dead guy they had to deal with.

Sirens swooped down to the wharf, bringing out the night owls, who began to form clusters around the bench. The SFPD soon had the situation in hand, taping off the area and keeping the looky-loos at a distance.

Sergeant Curtis approached them first. "You called this in, Brody?"

Curtis worked homicide with his brother. Ryan tucked Kacie against his side and extended his hand. "Good to see you, Sergeant. I missed you when I was at the department earlier today. This is Kacie Manning. She had a meeting with the guy, and I tagged along. We believe he's an ex-con named Duke Bannister."

"Kacie Manning." Curtis snapped his fingers. "You wrote that book on Daniel Walker—fascinating read."

Kacie peeled herself from Ryan's side and drew back her shoulders. "That's right. This man did time with Walker. He had some information for me, and that's why I was meeting him."

"Did either of you see anything out here?" Curtis swirled his finger in the air.

"No. I didn't realize Bannister was dead until I approached him from behind and touched his shoulder." She held out her hands. "I got his blood on my hands."

"We'll want to take a swab of that, Ms. Manning, and then you can clean up." He snapped his fingers for a tech.

"A transient came by soon after we discovered the body, but he claimed he hadn't seen anyone and then took off in a hurry. I, uh—" Ryan gestured toward Kacie "—had my hands full and couldn't detain him."

"No problem. A lot of these guys on the wharf are regulars. We'll have our guys put the word out. We'll offer an exchange of money for info. If someone saw something, the smell of cold hard cash usually brings them out of the woodwork. Do you think the information he had could've led to his murder, Ms. Manning?"

Kacie's eyes darted to Ryan's face and then back to Curtis's. "I'd met with Bannister before. He told me at that time Walker had it in for me."

Curtis whistled. "Do you think this is Walker's long hand from prison?"

"It could be."

Ryan joined in and told Curtis about the doll and how he'd dropped it off earlier today at the station. "Your lab guys have it now."

"We'll contact the warden at Walla Walla. He can have a little talk with Walker or more closely monitor his communications or do whatever he thinks necessary." Curtis leveled a finger at Ryan. "In the meantime, stay close to this guy. If you got a Brody on your side, you ain't doing half-bad."

After they answered a few more questions, a tech took a sample of blood from Kacie's hand, handed her a moist towelette and they were free to go.

Their shoulders bumped a few times on the walk back to the hotel. When the police showed up, Kacie seemed to have recovered, morphing back into the hard-nosed reporter.

And that was a good thing, but one part of him liked the way she clung to him, needed him. He wanted to be there for her.

She peppered him with questions and suggested likely scenarios all the way back to the hotel.

When the doors of the elevator slid open on the fourth floor, she held up her hand. "I'm okay, really."

"I know that, but what kind of cop would I be if I didn't see you safely to your room after the night you just had?"

She blinked. "I guess that sense of duty never goes away, does it? Even when you're off the clock."

"Funny thing about cops." He stepped out of the elevator and took her elbow. "We're never off the clock."

"I saw that with a lot of the men and women I interviewed for the book on Daniel Walker."

She'd allowed him to touch her, but that soft, yielding woman in his arms at the wharf had turned rigid and cold. If she wanted to keep this strictly business, he could comply.

When they reached her door, he dropped his hand. "Why do you think Walker had Bannister killed? Maybe he found out that Bannister already told you about his plan for revenge, so he killed him for punishment."

Folding her arms, she leaned against her door. "Or

maybe Bannister was about to give me more details about Walker's scheme, a scheme he didn't want revealed, something Walker may have told him in prison."

"It's in the warden's hands now."

She glanced down at her own palms, still stained with Bannister's blood despite the towelette. "My hands." Her gaze shifted to his shirt. "And your shirt. I'm so sorry. I ruined your shirt."

"This old thing?" He plucked the black T-shirt away from his chest. "I can toss it. It's seen better days."

And now it could die happy after having this woman pressed against it for five whole minutes.

"At least it's not soaked through. Is it?" She tapped a finger against the stiff cloth of his shirt.

"I don't think so." He pinched the hem of his shirt and yanked it up, exposing his stomach and chest. Dropping his chin to his chest, he said, "Nope. It didn't go through."

When he looked up, she dragged her gaze from his bare skin. A rosy color stained her cheeks and she expelled a quick breath through parted lips.

Good to see his charms held some fascination for her.

The shutters dropped over her eyes again and she made a turn for the door. "I'm going to scrub my hands with soap and water and get to bed. We have a busy day tomorrow."

He let his T-shirt fall. "Sweet dreams. I'll see you downstairs for breakfast at nine."

It took her three tries to unlock her door with Ryan still breathing down her neck, his muscles covered only by that thin black T-shirt.

When the green lights finally signaled success, she gave him a halfhearted wave and scurried inside the room, letting the door shut heavily behind her.

Why had she fallen into his arms so easily? Did she

have a choice? She'd just discovered a dead man awash in his own blood, for heaven's sake! She would've fallen into the arms of that homeless guy if he'd been handy. Ryan had just been handy.

But did handy have to feel so good?

She cranked on the water in the shower and stepped in. She cupped the little bar of soap in her hands as she held them beneath the warm stream. She lathered up her hands again and again, watching pink water swirl down the drain. The red from the scrubbing soon replaced the red from the blood. She toweled dry and dropped the towel to the bathroom floor.

Tomorrow she'd face the day with a fresh outlook. The warden at Walla Walla would handle Daniel Walker and get him off her back. Then she'd be free to pursue the Brody story.

Back on solid footing, she wouldn't need to run to the all-too-welcoming arms of Ryan every two seconds. Then she could get started on what she had come here to do—prove Joseph Brody's guilt as the Phone Book Killer beyond a reasonable doubt.

The following morning, she didn't even try to race Ryan downstairs. Let him have that petty victory. But as luck would have it, she beat him anyway. She took a table on the rim of the hotel restaurant and positioned her chair to face the lobby.

She generally liked to be waiting for her subject because she felt it gave her the upper hand, an opportunity to study her specimen before he knew he was being observed. In Ryan's case, it had the opposite effect.

As soon as he appeared in the lobby, her pulse quickened.

He exchanged a few words with the hotel clerk at the desk that had the clerk smiling from ear to ear. The hostess at the restaurant practically tripped over herself waving him to the table, and more than a few female heads turned as he threaded his way through the tables.

When he aimed that smile her way, Kacie experienced that newly familiar feeling of heat surging through her body and tingles spreading through her lady parts.

"Good morning. How'd you sleep?"

"Surprisingly well." To keep busy, she stirred way too much cream in her coffee. "Last night... Well, not that I'm happy someone is dead, but it's almost a relief to have Walker's threats out in the open. The warden can deal with him now."

He took his place across from her. "I wouldn't waste any tears on Bannister. The cops found two knives on him—one in his jacket pocket and one in his boot."

She choked on her sip of coffee. "He could've..."

"That's right. He could've been planning something for you. Maybe he didn't have any more information about Walker. Maybe he wanted to get close to you again."

"So, in a weird way, I owe Walker a debt of gratitude for getting rid of Duke Bannister."

"In a *really* weird way. I'm glad you're feeling better." He called the waiter over and ordered a cup of coffee.

"I'm ready to put all this behind me." She meant not only Walker and Bannister but also her insane attraction to Ryan Brody. She'd have to suppress that and get down to business.

"I hope you can. I hope the warden at Walla Walla deals with Walker." When his coffee arrived, he pointed to the cream next to her saucer. "Any of that left?"

She shoved it across to him. "We're going to take our first field trip to the Golden Gate Bridge. Are you okay with that?"

His spoon stopped short of his coffee and he sucked

in a quick breath. "I don't think we're going to find any evidence there."

"This first part—" she drew a circle on the table with her fingertip "—isn't about finding evidence. It's more about setting the mood. This has to be a story as well as just a report on the facts of the case. You know that, right?"

"I read your book." He rested his chin on top of his steepled fingers.

"I hope it's not going to be too hard on you." She laced her own fingers in her lap, resisting the ridiculous urge to caress his forearm.

"It won't be easy going through it all again, but if it proves my father's innocence, I'll walk through fire."

He may have to before this was all over because she planned to reveal his father as a killer. Then all this tension between them would blow up into smithereens.

They finished their breakfast and headed out to the parking structure where Ryan had left his car, a small SUV. He maneuvered through the streets of the city like a pro and pulled into the visitor parking for the bridge.

Kacie released her seat belt. "Where'd you learn to drive like that? I thought you lived in a little hick town up north?"

"I drove all around this city as a teenager. I wasn't always a hick." He winked at her.

"Hey, I'm not casting stones. The town I live in is no thriving metropolis."

He rested his hands on the steering wheel. "Did you grow up there?"

"My parents are in Seattle. I grew up there."

"And your sisters?"

"My sisters? How did you know I had sisters?" Her heart drummed a beat in her chest. Had he been checking up on her? How much could he have discovered through his police connections?

"Yesterday during our interview, you told me you had two older sisters."

"Oh yeah. One still lives in Seattle—married, children— and the other lives down in L.A., engaged." She'd have to watch her tongue around him.

She scrambled from the car and grabbed a light jacket from the backseat.

Shoving his hands into his pockets, he ambled to her side of the car and peered at the blue sky. "Not sure you're going to need that."

"It is a nice day, but it's always breezy on the bridge." She draped the jacket over her arm. "Ready?"

They crossed the parking lot and walked toward the pedestrian entrance. When they reached the walkway, tourists, cyclists and photographers joined them, while cars whizzed past on the road.

Ryan walked beside her, his head turned toward the bay. Did the view bring him pleasure, like it did most of the other pedestrians, or pain?

He stopped and grasped the low barrier, hunching his shoulders. "This is it."

She drew beside him, drinking in the view of Alcatraz and the city skyline floating between the blue of the bay and the blue of the sky. "This is a beautiful stop, but there are so many great views."

"No, I mean, this is it." The wind played with his hair, flattening it against his head as he looked down.

Then it hit her and her stomach dropped. "This is the exact spot where your father died?"

"This is where he jumped."

This time she did reach out, covering his hand with hers. "I'm sorry. We didn't have to… You didn't have to…"

He cranked his head around and his eyes blazed at her for a second. "You wanted to come here. You wanted to come and see where it all ended. Well, this is it. This is the spot."

A muscle twitched in her eye. Was he angry at her for foisting this on him? Ryan seemed like such an easygoing guy, but his hard mouth and harder eyes hinted at depths of rage she hadn't seen or expected.

Would this rage bubble over when he found out the truth?

By then she'd be far away, her lifelong goal reached. She brushed a wisp of hair from her face. "Do you want to leave?"

His shoulders dropped and he ran a hand through his thick, windblown hair. "No."

"His body was never found."

"Currents carried him out to sea."

"Were there any witnesses?"

"One." Turning sideways, he leaned on the barrier. "A woman was taking in the early-morning view. She'd noticed a man quite a distance from her. She watched as he climbed over the barrier and disappeared."

"She called the police?"

"She used one of the phones on the bridge to call the coast guard, but his body never turned up."

Kacie shivered despite the sun on her back. "Their station is so close I'm surprised they didn't find him."

"It happens. The current was swift that day. The police found my father's jacket and wallet on the ground and later they located his car in the parking lot—the same lot where we just parked."

"Have you or your brothers ever spoken to this witness?"

He cocked his head and pressed his back against the

barrier, spreading his arms along the top like a tourist posing for the camera. "I never have. If they did, they didn't tell me about it."

"I'd be curious to talk to her, if she's still alive. Do you know?"

"I know she was a young woman—early twenties."

"Do you remember her name?"

"I don't, but it would be in the case file for my father's suicide, and that's at the department."

"You can get your hands on that, right? You're the victim's son and you have connections."

"Uh-huh."

His gaze shifted away from her face and over her left shoulder. This visit had really affected him.

She cleared her throat. "I'd like to have a look at that file. Sometimes a fresh pair of eyes can yield some new insight."

"Uh-huh."

His eyes narrowed and his body tensed.

"Do you want to…?"

He swore and pushed past her.

As she stumbled, she twisted around just in time to see him lunge over the barrier—another Brody over the bridge.

Chapter Six

The barrier dug into his rib cage as he balanced on top of it, his hand grasping the straps of the woman's backpack.

"Don't do this."

She turned her head to look up at him with blank, red-rimmed eyes.

Kacie ran up beside him and dug her fingers into his arm. "What are you doing?"

"Call the cops from the phone. There's a woman on the ledge."

Kacie gasped and spun around.

The woman below him continued to stare at him, but she'd stopped struggling. She'd dropped to her knees on the steel ledge that ran almost the entire length of the bridge. There was nothing between her and a long drop into the choppy bay.

"Are you ready to come up now? Think about your family."

She sniffled and straightened up to her full height.

Ryan still held on to her backpack, but she could slip out of it at any second. He extended his other arm. "Grab on to me."

She glanced back at the endless sky in front of her, and Ryan's heart skipped a beat. Then she wrapped her hands around his arm.

He braced his feet against the barrier and hoisted her up and over it. She fell on top of him with a squeak, then rolled off him and curled into a fetal position on the ground.

Several pedestrians had watched the drama unfold. They formed a semicircle around him and the woman, who couldn't have been much older than twenty-five.

Kacie pushed through the onlookers. "The cops are on their way. I can see one coming on his bike."

The officer rode up with another officer right behind him. They dispersed the crowd and crouched beside the woman, who was still coiled into a ball.

Sirens followed, and the woman was lifted to her feet and bundled into the back of the squad car. The officer on the bike asked Ryan a few questions, got his name and number and pedaled off.

"Oh my God. I can't believe that happened right when we were here." She'd clapped a hand over her mouth and her eyes widened above it.

"It's a shame it happens at all. That woman was clearly in need of some help."

"Ryan Brody, you're such a hero. You put yourself in danger to save that stranger."

"Not at all. I was never in any danger of going over. She was small and light. Ask me if I'd have done it for some big bruiser."

Like Dad.

"I'm sure you would've tried. How often are people rescued from suicide attempts on the bridge?"

"I like to think more than are successful. The authorities try to keep a close eye on the activities up here."

"A closer watch than in your father's day."

"Definitely." He flexed his fingers, which had cramped up while holding on to the woman. "Now, let's get some lunch and visit the station for that case file. Unless you didn't get everything you needed here."

"Are you kidding? I got more than I bargained for." She touched his shoulder. "Thank you for coming here with me today. I see that it was difficult for you."

He stopped walking because he didn't want her to remove her hand from his arm, to scare her away. "Just because it's tough doesn't mean you flinch or turn away."

"Of course, if you hadn't been here, you wouldn't have saved that woman's life. She might not feel thankful now, but maybe she will later." She smoothed the material of his shirt before dropping her hand. "It all happened for a reason. Now, let's get that lunch."

Forty-five minutes later, Ryan took a big bite of his burger and mopped the grease from his chin as he watched Kacie stab an anemic piece of lettuce. "You sure do like your rabbit food."

"Some of us—" she waved her fork at him "—don't have time to spend hours in the gym or whatever you do to maintain that hard body."

She noticed? Did she take him for a gym rat, flexing in front of a mirror? "I have to stay physically fit for my job."

"Well, I don't." She added a tomato to the forkful of lettuce and popped it into her mouth.

"You don't need to be physically fit. You're physically fine." He didn't need a woman pumping iron alongside him. He preferred the contrast of a soft body next to his, and Kacie Manning had the kind of body a man could sink into.

Her cheeks reddened to match the tomatoes on her plate. "Are you going to follow up on that woman?"

"Yeah, I'll make a few calls, but they probably have her on a fifty-one-fifty hold. Maybe they can get her back on her meds and back on her feet, if that's what drove her to the bridge."

"It happens a lot, doesn't it? People jumping from the bridge?"

"About two or three times a month. And more attempts from people crying out for help."

"Like today. I don't think she was really going to jump. Do you?"

"I have no idea. I'd think if you're going to do it, you just do it, instead of hanging out on the ledge. I saw her slide over, and I thought she was gone, but she was crouched on the ledge."

"Exactly—it was a cry for help and you were there." She pushed back her chair and reached for her purse. "I'm going to use the ladies' room before we leave." She thumped her wallet on the table and slipped it open to a row of cards. She selected one and placed it on the table. "Use this for the check."

When she disappeared around the corner, he grabbed her card. He could at least pay for one of these meals.

He flipped open her wallet and it fell open to a plastic insert of pictures. A pretty young woman with coppery hair smiled at him from the plastic sheath.

He hunched over and studied the picture. The woman, with her voluptuous figure and full lips, resembled Kacie a lot more than the Nordic-looking family on her laptop.

A hand reached over his shoulder and smacked down on the wallet.

"What are you doing?"

He glanced up to meet Kacie's flashing brown eyes, their gold flecks throwing off sparks.

He held up his hands. "I'm not stealing your cash. Just the opposite. I was putting your card away. This lunch is on me for a change."

Her nostrils flared as she swept the wallet from the table and dropped it into her purse. "I told you. These meals are tax write-offs."

"Who's the woman in the picture? The one in the green dress?" He handed his credit card to the waiter.

"She's, uh, my grandmother when she was a young woman."

"I thought so."

Her eyebrows jumped. "You did?"

"I mean, not your grandmother, but I figured she was a relative. You look like her."

"She was my father's mother. She died young."

"Pretty lady."

"Thank you." She gulped the rest of her water and smiled brightly. "Ready to head to the station?"

Thirty minutes later, Ryan led the way into the hubbub of the big-city squad room. His brother had tried to lure him there a few times with job offers, but Ryan had preferred the peace and quiet of Crestview.

He stopped by Lieutenant Healy's office first. They shook hands and he introduced him to Kacie.

Healy's eyes lit up, but Ryan couldn't tell if it was from the way Kacie filled out her jeans or because he recognized the name.

"Kacie Manning—I enjoyed your book. Loved how you nailed that SOB Walker to the wall."

Okay, so maybe Ryan was the only one with impure thoughts about Kacie.

Kacie and the lieutenant shook hands. "I'm glad you appreciated that. Walker sure didn't."

"I got the lowdown from Curtis on that parolee's murder. We contacted the warden at Walla Walla. We'll let him handle Walker, but we still need to find out who did his dirty work."

"I hope you do because I think he's the same one who sent me a doll at Walker's bidding."

Healy puffed up his chest. "Don't worry. We'll nail him. You have other fish to fry right now, don't you?"

Ryan jabbed a finger at his own chest. "Are you calling me a fish?"

"Yeah, a shark." Healy wagged his finger at Kacie. "Don't let him fool you, Ms. Manning. He might come off as the carefree, easygoing brother, but all these Brody boys are harder than granite and just as uncompromising."

Ryan narrowed his eyes at Healy. The lieutenant and his brother didn't get along, and Ryan sensed that his animosity carried over to him.

"If you could keep me posted on Duke Bannister, I'd appreciate it—professional courtesy."

Healy shrugged. "Sure thing. How does your brother feel about this book?"

"All of my brothers are on board with it. We'd like to get to the bottom of what happened."

The lieutenant's lips spread into a mirthless smile. "Careful. You might not like what you find at the bottom of it all."

"We're willing to take that risk. As part of this—" he circled his finger in the air "—process, do I have permission to look up the case files?"

"*Mi casa es tu casa,* Chief. My house is yours."

He and Kacie moved toward the office door, and Ryan made a half turn in time to catch Healy checking out Kacie's derriere.

The lieutenant dragged his gaze up to Ryan's face. "Yes?"

"Any news on the attempted suicide this morning?"

"Oh yeah, I heard you were involved in that, too." He

sat down behind his desk and folded his hands. "She's on psych hold."

Ryan dropped his chin to his chest in a curt nod, then placed his hand on the small of Kacie's back to propel her out of the office.

As they walked to the elevator, Kacie leaned over to whisper in his ear. "Does he have something against you?"

"He doesn't like my brother Sean." He jabbed the elevator button. "Sean shows him up all the time. Makes him look bad. The lieutenant got written up a few months ago for not acting on a hunch of my brother's that turned out to be right. A woman got murdered because of it."

"Guess I should watch my back around him."

Yeah, because he's watching your backside.

Ryan sealed his lips and ushered Kacie into the elevator.

He didn't need to be her personal protector. She was a grown woman and had probably been handling unwanted male attention for years. She'd been handling his for the past few days.

He pushed the button for the basement.

"Next stop?" She folded her arms and wedged a shoulder against the elevator.

"Records."

The musty smell of the records lockup hit him as he opened the door, but the smell of a flowery perfume replaced it.

Marie Giardano peered at them through the mesh screen that guarded her counter, and her red lips broke into a wide smile. "If it isn't one of the Brody boys come to brighten up an old lady's day."

He strode across the room and curled his fingers around the edge of the screen. "You look as beautiful as ever."

She snorted but her eyes lit up. "You boys always say that, but you all come in here with other women in tow."

Ryan reached out and pulled Kacie toward the counter. "Marie Giardano, this is Kacie Manning. She's writing a book about Dad."

Marie pursed her lipsticked mouth into a straight line. "Really. You're the one who wrote that book on Daniel Walker, aren't you?"

"I am. Did you read it?"

"Nope." She jerked her thumb over her shoulder. "I get my fill of that stuff on the job. I stick to romance with a happily ever after."

Kacie blinked her eyes at Marie's hard tone.

"Kacie's going to find out the truth about Dad, Marie. She's going to set the record straight."

"Uh-huh." She turned back to Ryan. "What can I get for you? It's been a constant parade of Brody brothers this summer. When's that tough guy Judd going to pay his homage?"

"Judd's out of the country right now, but you can help me find the file on Dad's suicide."

"Really?" Her eyes slid from his face to Kacie's. "Why do you need to dig around in that?"

"I told you, Marie. Kacie's writing a book. We want to start with the end. We're going to try to find the woman who witnessed Dad jumping from the bridge that morning."

"Cookie Phelps."

"Cookie?"

"She was a hooker walking across the bridge that morning, probably after a night of seeing johns. Who knows? Maybe she was planning her own jump that morning."

"That's weird." His pulse ticked up a notch and he looked at Kacie to gauge her reaction.

Her eyes took up half her pale face and her breath quickened between parted lips.

She'd had a stronger reaction than he'd had to the identity of the witness.

Marie drummed her long nails on the counter. "What's weird about it? This city is full of hookers. Who else would be out and about at that time of the morning?"

"It's her presence on the bridge at precisely that time that's unusual. Chances are she was considering a jump. Why else would she be there? To sightsee? To take pictures in the dark?"

"So, maybe your father saved one more life before he died. Cookie saw him go over and changed her mind."

"She was interviewed?"

"Of course. She called it in."

"I want that file, Marie."

"If you can find it, you can check it out. Lieutenant Healy already phoned down with his blanket approval for any file you want."

She tapped on her keyboard and jotted down a few numbers on a slip of paper. "Here's the row and shelf."

"Thanks, Marie. Can I check it out or do I have to look at it here?"

"You can check that one out. It's just paper—no evidence." She buzzed the cage open, and Ryan held the door open for Kacie.

Kacie smiled her thanks at Marie, who had already turned back to her computer.

When they got to the row in the back of the room, Kacie trailed her hand along the boxes, reading out the numbers. She turned abruptly, almost running into his chest. "She doesn't like me much, does she?"

"Didn't seem like it. Maybe it's just the claws coming out from one femme fatale to another." He winked.

Rolling her eyes, she said, "She knew your father?"

"She was good friends with my father and mother. After

Dad died, Marie would drink with my mom, just to see her home safely." He located the box and pulled it from the shelf. "She probably just doesn't like the idea of a book coming out and dredging up painful old memories."

He balanced the box on a rolling stool and flipped off the lid. "There's not too much in here. I'm just going to take the whole box if Marie lets me."

"That woman would let you get away with murder."

"She's loyal, but not that loyal."

"Figure of speech, Brody." She replaced the lid and smacked her fist against it.

Ryan hoisted the box in his arms, and Kacie led the way out of the maze of metal shelves stuffed with cold cases. The files for the Phone Book Killer were there somewhere, and he was sure they'd get to those in due time.

Marie looked up from her keyboard. "Got what you need?"

"Right here." Ryan patted the side of the box. "We'll return it tomorrow."

"Take your time, and send Judd over when he returns to U.S. soil."

"Will do."

"Thanks. Nice to meet you, Marie." Kacie waved as she held the door open for Ryan and the box.

Marie flicked her long fingernails in their general direction.

"Oh boy." Kacie pulled the door closed with a click.

Twenty minutes later, when they reached the elevator of their hotel, Ryan's finger hovered between two buttons. "Your room or mine?"

"Let's stick to my room. It's closer."

Clutching the box to his chest, he waited while Kacie opened her door. She stepped inside the room and wedged her foot against the door to hold it open for him.

He squeezed past her into the room, and she sucked in a breath. He dropped the box to the floor by the window and pulled out the two bulging file folders. Then he walked to the table and placed them side by side. "Lotta stuff here for one suicide."

Kacie joined him at the table and spun one of the folders around to face her. "No wonder. This is for a different case—domestic violence."

"Someone misfiled something." He dropped the extra folder back into the box and thumbed open his father's case.

Kacie placed a hand on his forearm. "Are you sure you're up to this? I can go through it myself."

He covered her hand with his. "Do you think I lost it on the bridge?"

"It upset you, being in that spot, and I don't blame you."

"It was eerie, but don't you think I've been there before? As soon as I was old enough to take the Muni to the bridge, I checked it out."

"I can certainly understand that, but if you'd prefer not to look at this file…"

"It's just words on paper. It's not like the coast guard ever found his body and took pictures."

She disengaged her hand from his and pulled her chair to his side of the table. "Okay, then. Let's take this from the top."

Facing her laptop, she pushed it back on the table. The movement woke up the display, and Kacie jerked her head up and gasped.

His gaze darted from the blue screen to Kacie's tight face. "What's wrong?"

"Someone's been in my room."

Chapter Seven

Ryan's body tensed and he looked ready to tackle someone. That was what she liked about him—he was always ready.

"How do you know? Is something missing?"

"It's my laptop." She jabbed a finger at the blue display with the log-in prompt glowing white against it. "When my computer goes to sleep, it displays my screen saver, that picture of my parents. The log-in prompt stays there only after several incorrect log-in attempts."

He pushed back from the table. "You're sure?"

"That's how I configured it, or at least that's how the self-described computer geek in my apartment building configured it."

"Look around. Is anything else different? Missing?"

She hopped up from the chair and took a turn around the room. Everything seemed as it was. She yanked open the dresser drawers and poked her head in the closet. She flipped on the lights in the bathroom and ran her hand along the vanity. She called over her shoulder. "I don't see anything different."

"Are you sure about the laptop?"

"Yes."

"You know how computers are. They act up, have glitches."

"Are you trying to convince me someone *wasn't* in my room?"

"There's no other evidence."

"This isn't a case you have to bring to the D.A., Chief Brody. I just have a feeling."

"But you didn't have this feeling until you saw something unexpected on your computer. Do you also have a feeling it's Walker?"

"Maybe the warden had a talk with him, but Walker hasn't gotten the word to his minion yet to lay off."

"You said failed log-in attempts. So let's say Walker's minion was in here. Did he fail to log in to your computer?"

"Yes." She entered her password and her folders popped up on her desktop display.

"Why would Walker want to get in to your computer?"

"Just to mess with me, Ryan. Put me on edge."

"Do you want to call hotel security?"

"I wouldn't know what to report. I don't even know what this guy looks like. Walker wouldn't send someone who stands out into a hotel. He wouldn't get past the front desk."

"Why don't you check your files to make sure everything's okay?"

She did a cursory check through her folders, which she backed up every day anyway, and again nothing was amiss.

"Okay, maybe it was a computer glitch, but next time I leave the room I'm going to put some trigger in place, a thread across the door or something."

"Maybe you need a full-time bodyguard. Too bad my brother's out of town."

She looked at him through her lashes. She already had one Brody looking out for her.

Finding nothing else, they returned to the file on the suicide, reading aloud snippets of paragraphs.

Kacie tapped a pencil against the page. "It was foggy that night. I'm wondering if Cookie was closer than she claimed to be."

"Why would you think that?"

"You know how it can get on the bridge with the fog rolling in. Sometimes you can't see your hand in front of your face, and yet Cookie saw a man throw himself over the barrier from twenty feet away."

"What's your point? Why would she lie about her location?"

"I don't know. Maybe she was close enough to stop him and didn't do anything. Then felt guilty about it later."

"Maybe." He folded the corner of that page and flipped to the next. "She used one of the emergency phones on the bridge to call—no cell phones back then."

"The coast guard responded within two minutes of the call and didn't find a thing. The police questioned Cookie and then let her slide back into oblivion. She certainly didn't seek the limelight or her fifteen minutes of fame."

"I wonder if she went back to hooking." He dragged her laptop toward them. "I'm going to search for Cookie and see if she's still in the city."

Kacie continued to thumb through the file as Ryan worked his magic on her computer. She'd have to remember how easy it was working with a cop. They had inroads that she and her P.I. could only dream of.

"This is interesting."

She hunched forward. "What?"

"Looks like Cookie got out of the life after my father's death."

"Maybe it scared her straight."

"Really straight. She's working as a Realtor now."

"Good for Cookie. Is her name still Cookie?"

"She's using her real name now, Cynthia Phelps."

"I'm sure she sells a lot more homes with that name." She drew her brows together and clicked her fingernail against the table.

"Why so thoughtful? Are you thinking of investing in real estate now?"

"Phelps. That name sounds familiar."

"Maybe you saw one of her signs. They'll make it easier to locate her."

She snapped her fingers and lunged for the box. "Phelps—the domestic-violence case."

She yanked the folder out of the box and smacked it against the table. Swirls of dust danced along the beams of sunlight coming through the windowpane.

She ran her finger down the first page. "Yep. Cynthia Phelps called the cops on her boyfriend, Frankie Lawson."

"At least that explains how the file got dropped in with this one—witness in one case, complainant in the other." Ryan stretched and then laced his fingers behind his head.

Kacie continued to skim the file. Her finger ran across the name of the arresting officer and then moved back. Her mouth fell open. "Ryan."

"What?"

"You're not going to believe this."

"Let me guess. Frankie was her pimp."

"That may be, but there's something else—Joseph Brody was the arresting officer."

"What?" Ryan dropped his hands and snatched the file from her. He held the paper close to his face and swore. "What are the chances of that?"

"It's such a coincidence. This arrest happened years before the suicide, before your father was a homicide detective."

"Now we really have to track her down and talk to her." He smacked the file onto the table. "I wonder if she even recognized my father as the cop who came out to her place."

"Where did you say she works now?"

He spun the laptop around to face him. "Bay Realtors. I think we need to look at an open house today."

KACIE LEANED FORWARD in the passenger seat of Ryan's car, her nose almost touching the windshield. "Looks like that couple is heading out."

"I hope they made Cookie an offer to put her in a good mood." He slipped the key from the ignition. "She probably doesn't want to be reminded of her past now that she has a squeaky-clean life."

"That's why it's best we do this here, away from a possible husband and her squeaky-clean home."

They approached the house, located in the Sunset District, and tapped on the open door as they crossed the threshold.

Kacie called out. "Hello?"

An attractive blonde with a neat pencil skirt and a tucked-in blouse showcasing her slim figure emerged from the kitchen, carrying a plate of chocolate-chip cookies.

She smiled. "Hello. Just in time for a fresh batch. Would you like one?"

"No, thank you." Kacie stepped away from the table so Cynthia could put the plate down.

"I'll have one." Ryan selected a cookie from the plate and bit off half, the warm, gooey chocolate melting in his mouth.

He saw Kacie trying to catch his eye, probably to see if he recognized the significance in Cookie offering cookies, but he avoided her smirk.

"Do you prefer to look around on your own or would you like me to show you the place?"

"Actually, Cynthia—" Ryan plucked a napkin from the white tablecloth and dusted his fingertips "—we're here to talk to you about something else."

Cynthia's eye twitched and she smoothed her skirt with nervous hands. The life clearly still haunted her.

"Who are you?"

He reached into his pocket and pulled out his badge. "I'm Chief Ryan Brody. Yeah, *that* Brody. And this is Kacie Manning. She's a writer doing a book on my dad. You knew my dad, didn't you, Cynthia?"

She folded her hands in front of her, her white knuckles almost matching her cream-colored skirt. "Of course I knew Joseph Brody. He was a good man."

"A good man who you saw jump off the Golden Gate Bridge."

"That's right." She lifted her chin. "I didn't know it was Joey Brody at the time. If I had known, maybe I could've done something to stop him."

"So you're saying you didn't find out it was Joseph Brody who'd jumped off the bridge until later?"

"That's right." Her gaze darted toward the front door as if she were planning an escape from her own open house. "The cops never even told me. I read about it along with everyone else."

"When you found out it was Detective Brody, it must've been a…shock." Kacie touched Cynthia's arm in a sympathetic gesture.

"I was even more upset when I found out who it was." Cynthia grabbed the edge of the tablecloth and twisted it between her fingers. "Joey Brody saved my life once. If I had known that was him on the bridge, I would've done anything to save his life. Anything."

"Did the cops at the time make the connection between you and my father? Did they realize he'd arrested your pimp several years before?"

Glancing over her shoulder, she said, "No. They didn't know, or at least they didn't ask me about it. When I read the story in the newspaper, I didn't bother telling them. I was still in the life. I didn't need to remind the cops about that."

Kacie picked up a cookie from the plate and broke it in two, showering crumbs on the tablecloth. "What were you doing on the bridge at that time of the morning, Cynthia?"

She dropped the tablecloth and began picking at the cuticles of her manicured nails. "It wasn't closed to pedestrians. I was just walking, like anyone else."

"At the break of dawn? In the fog?"

"It's not against the law." She pulled back her shoulders and brushed the crumbs from the table into a napkin, which she then crumpled in her fist. "What do you want from me, Chief Brody? I never saw your father's face that morning. I didn't talk to him. He didn't say a word. One minute there was a man on the bridge through the fog. The next, that man had hoisted himself over the ledge, like so many before him and so many since. I told you. I would've given my own life to save your father's."

Ryan took her cold hand in his and she jerked back. He rested the pad of his thumb against her racing pulse. "I don't want anything from you, Cynthia. I just wanted to look at the woman who was the last person to see my father alive. I think my dad would've been pleased that it was you—someone he had helped in another life."

Tears flooded her blue eyes, eyes that had seen too much. "Just so you know, I never believed any of that stuff about your father. He was no killer. I guess it all just got to be too much for him. Sometimes it just gets to be too much."

"I appreciate that." Ryan squeezed her hand. "My brothers and I don't believe it, either, and neither does Ms. Manning. That's what this book is all about. We're going to clear his name."

A commotion at the front door signaled another set of potential buyers. Cynthia whispered, "Be careful," and she yanked her hand away from his as she greeted the newcomers.

Ryan pocketed one of Cynthia's cards and grabbed Kacie's elbow to steer her out the door. "Thanks, Cynthia. We're interested and we'll talk to our Realtor about an offer."

When they hit the sidewalk, Kacie spun around. "What was that about?"

"Just trying to help her out. If those people think there are other interested buyers, it might light a fire under them."

As she shook her head, the sun glinted off the copper strands in her hair. "Not that. She told us to be careful. What did she mean?"

"You heard that, too?" Ryan rubbed his knuckles across his chin. "I thought I'd imagined it."

"Why would she say that?" Kacie paced away from him, tossed her cookie halves in the gutter and made her way back, poking her finger against his chest. "And why was she so nervous?"

"She's a former hooker running from her past. Why wouldn't she be nervous around a cop? Or two people showing up while she's trying to do her job and questioning her about her old life?"

"It was more than that, Ryan, and you know it. She's

hiding something about that night—or rather, that morning."

He took her hand and pulled her toward the car parked at the curb. "Maybe it's like we were speculating before. She was there to jump, saw someone else jumping and had a change of heart."

"Then later found out the person who had jumped was the cop who'd intervened in her conflict with her pimp, probably saving her life. It sounds so unlikely. Maybe he arranged to meet her there that morning."

"What are you implying, Kacie? My father had Cookie join him at the bridge to make sure he had a witness? I don't think he'd do that to her."

Leaning against the car, she placed her hands on his shoulders. "Is that why you're denying the coincidences in her story? You're afraid it'll make your dad look cold and unfeeling?"

"I don't know." He ducked his head, pinching the bridge of his nose. "You're right. Cynthia was agitated. Why did she keep saying she'd have done anything to save my father?"

"Maybe he did have her meet him there to witness the jump. She agreed to help him out and then felt guilty about it. Maybe she knew why he'd called her there." She smoothed the cotton of his T-shirt against his shoulders, and then she folded her arms over her chest. "There's something not quite right about the whole scenario."

He cranked his head over his shoulder to take in the for-sale sign. "We should question her again."

"I agree, but that's not going to happen right now while she's showing a house. If she sees us out here waiting for her, she'll never let that couple go."

"Right again." He walked around to the passenger side of the car and opened the door. "Let's give her some breathing room."

Ryan didn't have much to say on the ride back to the hotel. Throughout the conversation with Cynthia, he'd felt as if there was another subtext to her words. What had she been trying to tell him? He slid a glance at Kacie in the passenger seat. And would she be more willing to tell him if he questioned her alone?

He parked the car, and they entered the hotel elevator. When they stopped at Kacie's floor, Ryan held the door open and said, "Do you want me to come with you to your room in case your trigger has shifted?"

Before Kacie had walked away from her room, she'd placed a toothpick against her door. He'd kept trying to tell her that anyone on a hotel hallway could knock it over without necessarily opening the door of her room, but she seemed to think the trick would work well enough.

"I can always use a little backup."

She crooked her finger at him. He would've followed her anywhere. When they reached her door, she crouched down. "The toothpick is still leaning against the door."

"Same spot? Someone could've noticed it and replaced it."

"It's in the same spot. I counted the threads of carpet from the doorjamb."

"Where do you learn this stuff?" He held out his hand and she dropped the toothpick into his palm.

"Where anyone learns anything these days—the internet."

"Dinner later, or are you going to stick to your room again?" He tossed the toothpick from hand to hand, practicing his nonchalant look.

"I'm up for a working dinner—say, seven o'clock?"

A working dinner beat a pathetic table for one and a pay-per-view movie. "Lobby at seven o'clock."

She shut the door on Ryan and the toothpick and did a

quick survey of the room. Nothing was out of place, but she still felt on edge.

Maybe it was that whole interview with Cynthia Phelps. The fact that she'd already had an association with Joseph Brody and then happened to be on the bridge to witness his jump was weird enough, but add to that her jittery manner at the open house and one plus one was definitely adding up to something more than two.

She sat on the edge of the bed and kicked off her shoes. She'd meant what she'd said to Ryan about a working dinner. If she kept her mind on work, it would leave less room for her emotional response to him and his hot body.

And that was all it was. He was a good-looking guy with juicy slabs of muscle. Any woman could appreciate that, but it didn't require any action on her part. She sucked in her bottom lip and then bit it.

Stop thinking about him in that way.

She had a job to do—prove Joseph Brody's guilt—and no sexy son or loyal friends would deter her. Both Marie Giardano and Cynthia Phelps had Joey Brody's back, and neither one of them seemed all too pleased with her or the prospect of her book.

They knew him, or thought they knew him, and wanted to protect him. Even Daniel Walker had his defenders, and every serial killer in lockup had enjoyed marriage proposals from the outside.

Kacie stepped out of her clothes and tossed them on the closet floor. She showered and changed into a skirt to keep the dinner professional. Of course, the skirt was a flowery number that hit about midthigh.

Biting the inside of her cheek, she turned in front of the mirror to check the back view. She reached for the waistband when a knock on her door made her jump.

She peered through the peephole to see Ryan waving. He was taking this punctuality thing way too far.

Glancing down at her bare chest, she swept a T-shirt from the bed and pulled it over her head. She opened the door a crack. "You're early."

"I dropped by to pick up the file on my dad's suicide. There was something I wanted to check before dinner."

She widened the door and made a sweeping gesture with her arm. "Enter. It's on the table where we left it. I'm still getting ready."

He squeezed past her into the room, checking her out from head to bare toes. "I'm glad you're not done getting dressed. I'm no fashion expert, but that shirt doesn't go with the skirt."

"Thank you for your advice, Mr. Givenchy." She plucked at the hem of her skirt and curtsied.

Ryan cocked his head. He sauntered to the desk and scooped up the folder. "You're getting a call."

She held up her hands and he tossed the buzzing cell phone at her. Cupping the phone in her hand, she read Unknown Number on the display. The unknown was nothing unusual in her line of work.

She answered. "Hello?"

"Why, hello, Kacie. This is Daniel Walker."

Chapter Eight

The low voice as smooth as a sharp blade sent a cascade of shivers down her back and she dropped to the edge of the bed. She'd never shown one ounce of weakness to Walker, and she wasn't about to start now. "How are you calling me?"

Ryan jerked his head up from the file and mouthed the words *What's wrong?*

Had the fear seeped into her tone? She cleared her throat and put her cell on Speaker.

Walker chuckled. "It's called a phone."

Ryan's brows collided over the bridge of his nose as he crossed the room in two steps and crouched beside the bed.

"You know what I mean, Walker." She met Ryan's eyes and dipped her chin as his mouth formed an O. "How is it you have access to a phone to call me?"

"All things are possible in prison, Kacie, my dear."

"The cops will be onto you if you decide to send your thug after me again."

He clicked his tongue and even that sound caused her to clench her jaw. "Kacie, Kacie, that's why I'm calling. The warden had a little chat with me and I assured him, like I'm assuring you now, I never sent anyone after you. I'm an innocent man, biding my time and preparing for my appeal."

"B.S." She bounded up from the bed, nearly knocking Ryan over, and paced to the window. "Duke Bannister warned me that you were coming for me, and then you had him killed."

"Who's Duke Bannister? Sounds like a boxer."

"He was a fellow inmate of yours at Walla Walla." She licked her lips. "Just stop it. You know who Bannister is."

"I'm afraid I've never had the…pleasure of meeting Mr. Bannister. Or does he prefer Duke?"

"He doesn't prefer anything now. He's dead."

"So, an ex-con comes out of nowhere claiming to know me and proceeds to warn you that I'm after you? Sounds perfectly logical to me." Walker coughed.

"Yeah, he warned me, and then I got locked in the hotel sauna, and I got that doll."

As the silence on the other line dragged on, she shrugged at Ryan. Maybe Walker had been busted for the phone use.

"Hello?"

"What doll?"

"Someone sent me a doll just like the one your daughter had. I got the message."

She heard Walker begin to sob and the sound had her bobbling the phone. She closed her eyes, fighting the sympathy that surged through her body. He didn't deserve it.

She heard shouts over the phone and then a harsh whisper from Walker. "It wasn't me. I didn't do it. I wouldn't do it."

Then the line went dead.

Planting her hands on the table on either side of her laptop, Kacie hunched over, the phone still clutched in one fist.

She felt the warmth of Ryan's presence behind her and then his strong fingers squeezing her shoulder.

"Are you okay?"

She took a deep breath and turned to face him, close enough for her breasts beneath the baggy T-shirt to brush against his chest. Close enough to see his green eyes changing color at the contact. "I'm fine. He's so good, so convincing, isn't he?"

"What do you think he meant at the end? He didn't kill his family, or he didn't have someone stalk you?"

"I don't know—probably both. To deny the one is to deny the other. If he never killed his family, he wouldn't be the type to go after me for proving he did. Threatening me would almost be like admitting his guilt—and he'll never do that, not as long as he has breath in his lungs."

"He seemed really broken up about his daughter."

"He's a good actor."

"Why would he go through the trouble of contacting you to tell you he wasn't threatening you?"

She shuffled away from him and peered out the window at the darkening street below. "I don't pretend to know what goes through the man's mind."

"Really? Because in the book you sort of did pretend to know what was going through his mind. Think about it. If he did discuss his plans with Bannister and then send someone to carry them out, why would he direct attention to himself by calling you, especially after the warden already talked to him about Bannister's murder?"

She yanked on the rod of the drapes. "He enjoys the attention, Ryan. He saw it as another opportunity to maintain his innocence to me."

"If you say so." He shrugged.

"Besides, I don't have any other enemies. Who else would be locking me in saunas and sending me dolls? Bannister was offed for warning me about Walker."

"Was he?"

"Of course. What are you talking about?" She folded her

arms over her stomach, grabbing handfuls of the T-shirt on both sides.

"You were going to meet him that night because he'd called you at lunch and said he had something to tell you."

"Yeah?"

"He'd already warned you about Walker. What more did he have to say?"

"Maybe he was going to tell me something about the doll." She bit her bottom lip, not enjoying the direction of the conversation.

"Why would he do that? If he even knew about the doll, he'd know that you'd figure out he was telling you the truth about his warning. What more would he have to say?"

"So what's your theory?"

"He was going to tell you the truth—that someone besides Walker had sent him."

She threw up her hands. "You're basing all this on Walker's insistence that he didn't do it. They all say that, don't they?"

"I'm just playing devil's advocate here." He tucked the file under his arm. "I still want to look this over. You can finish getting dressed, and I'll meet you downstairs in fifteen minutes."

He jogged up the stairwell to work off some tension. Kacie hadn't been wearing a bra beneath that T-shirt. She may have thought it was loose-fitting, but every time she moved, the soft material conformed to her breasts, making it hard to concentrate on the conversation...or just making it hard.

When he got to his room, he splashed some cold water on his face and brushed his teeth. Then he stretched out on the bed and skimmed through the file on his father's suicide again, flipping to the back pages.

At the time of his father's suicide, Cookie Phelps had

been a streetwalker, plying her trade in the Tenderloin and turning over most of her earnings to a pimp. How had she broken out of that cycle? Where had she gotten the money to attend real-estate classes and take the test for her license?

That had all happened in quick succession, shortly after his father's death. According to her website, Cynthia Phelps had been a Realtor for almost twenty years.

Had one event influenced the other? The thought that his father may have made some arrangement with Cynthia left a bad taste in his mouth.

He checked the time and stashed the file in the nightstand drawer. He'd bring all this up with Kacie at dinner. Maybe she could arrange to wear a potato sack, because that was the only way he was going to be able to focus on anything other than not peeling off her clothes.

No such luck.

The sway of her hips as she approached him in the lobby made the flounces of her skirt twitch back and forth. She'd replaced the baggy T-shirt with a V-neck sweater, and although she had her breasts properly ensconced in a bra, there was nothing proper about the way the soft material of the sweater hugged her assets.

He closed his mouth and hoped the drool hadn't made it to his chin.

Standing up at her approach, he smiled. "That sweater is a much better match."

"I'm glad you approve. I feel so much better about my selection now."

He pointed to her feet in a pair of low-heeled sandals. "Can you walk in those? I'm thinking seafood at the Wharf."

"No problem. I don't feel like battling traffic and searching for a decent place to park. Let's skip the big touristy places."

"Agreed."

They stepped into the cool night and Kacie threw a light jacket over her shoulders.

"Let's beat the light." Ryan grabbed her hand and pulled her into the crosswalk as the red hand blinked at them.

"You like living dangerously, don't you?" She freed her hand from his on the pretext of clutching the collar of her jacket. "Drivers in this city are an impatient bunch."

"You seem to know San Francisco well. Do you spend a lot of time here?"

"I…" She fussed with her jacket, finally shoving her arms through the sleeves. "I come here a few times a year—meetings, book signings. I like it."

"Do you like it better than Seattle?"

"Both cities have their charms." She stopped at the curb and smacked her palm against the light for the signal. "How about you? Do you miss it?"

"Crestview isn't that far away, and two of my brothers are here, so I come in at least once a month." He touched her elbow and pointed to the right. "This way."

Hunching her shoulders, she said, "I'm glad you said that. Bannister was killed in the other direction. Do the police have any leads in the case?"

"If they do, they're not telling me." He guided her around a crowd of people watching a man dressed up like a robot, his face caked with silver makeup. "But I'm calling the lieutenant tomorrow to let him know about Walker's call."

"Oh." She rubbed her nose. "Do you think that's necessary?"

"He's not supposed to be calling you, Kacie. He'd been warned. How does he have your number, anyway?"

"We were in very close contact at one time. I guess he kept my number."

He shook his head. "You never changed your number after giving it to a psychopath like Walker? Come to think of it, how did Bannister get your number?"

"I gave it to him after he emailed me from my website. With the type of writing I do, I need to keep the lines of communication open. It's a risk I'm willing to take to get and keep my contacts."

"Talk about living dangerously." He opened the door of the restaurant for her but felt like wrapping her in his arms instead. She might see herself as a tough cookie dealing with these criminals, but they saw her as an easy mark.

After the waiter brought their drinks and food, Ryan settled back in the booth and wrapped his hands around the chilly mug of beer. When Kacie pulled her mini-recorder from her purse, he groaned. "You're kidding."

She cocked her head. "I told you it was a working dinner."

"I didn't believe you."

"Why wouldn't you believe me? Did you think I'd need time to recover just because Walker called?"

"It's okay if you do." He flicked her wineglass with his finger, and the golden liquid inside shimmered in the candlelight. "I don't mind a little business with my pleasure, but can we do this without the recorder?"

She swept it back into her purse. "Done. Did you discover anything else from that file after you left my room?" she asked as she picked up her fork and dug into her salad.

"Just that Cookie turned her life around shortly after my father's suicide. She went from streetwalker to house seller in record time."

"Maybe the tragedy inspired her to do something more with her life."

"Possibly, but it takes some quick money to turn your life around like that."

"Are you suggesting she got it from your father?"

Ryan took a bite of his food and a long swallow of his beer, then placed the mug on the table. "I hate to even think it, but it sure seems like a coincidence that she winds up with the means to change her life after witnessing Dad's suicide."

"That's one proposition I would've liked to have heard."

"Maybe Cookie didn't know why he'd asked her to join him on the bridge."

"Why would he even want a witness? Wouldn't leaving his personal effects on the bridge be proof enough that he had jumped?"

"I don't know, Kacie. Maybe we're just reading way too much into Cookie's presence on the bridge. She was there, and she saw him, a cop who had arrested her pimp. Maybe it was what it was—a coincidence.

"I'm not sure questioning her again will do any good, but I might give it a try anyway." He dropped his napkin on the table. "The discovery of Cookie does indicate there's a lot of untapped information on my father's case. Who knows what more we'll find out when we start going through the case files—witnesses, suspects, victims."

Kacie slammed the glass she'd been drinking from on the table, and the water sloshed over the rim. "Sorry. You know, Ryan, I'm not sure we need to delve into all of that. This is more of a personal story from your perspective."

"Really?" He tapped his unused spoon against the table. "I thought the point of this book was to prove my father's innocence. That's why I signed on."

"And I think we can do that by telling your story."

"It's not my story, Kacie." He cocked his head. "It's

my father's story, and to get it right we need to burrow into the past."

She threaded her fingers together. "We'll have to dig into the case file after we pick it up from Records when we drop off the suicide file. Maybe we can split it up. I'll take the victims, and you can have…whatever."

"Yeah, and the best part is we don't even have to go back to Records to muddle through the stuff. My brother's fiancée made copies of everything in the case file and organized it."

"Even the pictures?"

"Everything."

"That's great." Kacie glanced at her phone. "Can we get going?"

"Dessert?"

"No, thanks." She pressed her fingers to her temples. "I'm not feeling that great."

She didn't even make a move for her wallet to pay for the dinner. He placed his own card on the table and covered her fidgeting fingers with his hand. "We'll take a taxi back to the hotel."

"That's okay. I could use the fresh air." She waved her fingers in the air to get the waiter's attention. "Where are these cataloged and organized notes?"

"In my hotel room. My brother Eric gave them to me before he went back to D.C."

"That's convenient." She took a sip of water and closed her eyes. Then she pulled in a long breath and straightened her shoulders. "Not sure if I'm up for any more work tonight. Maybe my body's trying to tell me to take it easy."

"Then let's get out of here so you can…take it easy."

By the time he'd paid the bill and they stepped out into the cool night, Kacie had gotten her color back.

"You're feeling better?" He adjusted her jacket around

her shoulders, and his fingertips brushed the smooth skin stretched across her collarbone.

Her eyes met his, and her lips parted. "I feel...fine."

She wriggled deeper into her jacket, and he had to stuff his hands into his pockets to keep from pulling her lush body into his arms.

"Great. If you start feeling lousy again, let me know."

She hooked her arm through his, pressing her shoulder against his shoulder. "What'll you do? Sweep me up in your arms again and carry me back to my room?"

The scent of her perfume and her soft hair tickling his chin overwhelmed his senses. Was she coming on to him? She'd been holding him at arm's length up to that point, despite his broad hints that she pushed his buttons in all the right ways. Maybe it was just because she'd been feeling faint. Once she came to her senses, she'd probably push him away again and insist on professionalism. So, should he take advantage of her momentary lapse of professionalism?

He left his hands in his pockets. "If you collapse on the sidewalk, I'll definitely call an ambulance."

"Oh, that's comforting." She rubbed her cheek against his shoulder like a satisfied cat.

This time the strands of her hair caught on his beard. He pulled one hand out of his pocket and curled his arm around Kacie's waist. He waited for her to pull away or engage with some distraction, like her phone.

She snuggled against him, her curves fitting against the hard lines of his body.

He tightened his hold, his fingertips sinking into the swell of her hip.

They strolled down the sidewalk, side by side, fitting in with all the couples on their date nights.

They stopped to watch the robotic man. Kacie pulled a dollar bill from her purse and dropped it into his bucket.

"Is that tax-deductible, too?"

She laughed, a warm, sultry sound that made him feel as if they shared some deep secret that set them apart from everyone else around them.

"No, it is not." Then she smacked his backside, allowing her fingers to linger and brush against the denim.

She'd better not have been teasing, because she'd just made him hard past the point of no return.

As their hotel rose before them, Ryan grabbed Kacie's hand and quickened his steps. When they hit the elevator, he punched the buttons for both floors. His room, her room—he didn't care where this happened.

But she apparently had a preference. When the doors opened on her floor, she punched the button to close the doors. When the car hit his floor, he took one step off the elevator, straddling the door, and she brushed past him into the hallway.

She glanced over her shoulder. "Are you coming?"

When she looked at him like that, he had every intention of coming. He followed her provocatively swaying hips toward his room and shoved his key card in the slot while she wedged a shoulder against the door.

He pushed open the door, and she fell into the room. He caught her shoulders and pulled her close, gazing into her liquid brown eyes.

Her lashes fluttered and she ran her tongue along her lips.

His tongue followed suit before he plunged it into her warm mouth. She closed around him and took a step closer, pressing her breasts against his chest, hooking one arm around his waist.

He let the door slam behind them and then deepened his kiss as he placed both hands on her derriere, pulling her close and fitting her against his pelvis.

She gasped into his mouth, her body going limp.

He backed her up against the wall and yanked the jacket from her shoulders. As it fell to the floor, he slid down the zipper of her skirt.

He didn't even have to pull it off. It joined the sweater on the floor. He ran one hand up her smooth thigh and traced the line of her panties with his fingertip.

She squirmed against him, but he had other plans. He grabbed the edge of her sweater and tugged it up. She raised her arms and he pulled it over her head and tossed it over his shoulder.

Her breasts, encased in a lacy black bra, heaved with her panting breath. With each expansion of her lungs, the flimsy lace could barely contain the smooth, milky flesh. The bra hooked in the front, making his life a whole lot easier. With one little twist, he unhooked the bra and Kacie's breasts spilled into his greedy hands.

He cupped them in his palms and ran the pads of his thumbs across her rosy, peaked nipples.

She hissed and threw her head back, banging it against the wall.

As he rolled one nipple between his thumb and forefinger, he dipped his head to suck on the other. At the contact, her hips lunged against his, and he grabbed a handful of her luscious backside to steady her.

He teased her nipple with his tongue and lips, blowing on it gently while he pinched her other nipple.

The sensations drove Kacie wild with desire.

Moaning, she thrashed her head from side to side and curled one leg around his denim-clad calf.

Her hands clawed at his T-shirt. He'd stripped her down to her panties and he still had every bit of clothing on. How had that happened? She'd planned to seduce him in a controlled manner, keeping him on a tight leash, and she'd wound up quivering, almost naked, against the wall.

He grabbed her hands with one of his, cinching her wrists together over her head as he continued focusing his attention on her breasts.

The tender suckling of the one contrasted with the almost painful tweaking of the other until she couldn't distinguish the pleasure from the pain and they merged into one overwhelming sensation of need.

She tried loosening her hands from his grip, but once she got them free, he flattened his solid body against hers. One hand came up behind her and yanked her panties down around her thighs.

He cupped her bottom and extended his fingers between her legs, thrusting them into her wet folds.

She whimpered. It was all she could manage.

His suckling of her breast became more insistent, alternating with and matching the thrusting of his fingers.

The dual attack made it hard for her to breathe, hard for her to think, hard for her to remember why she'd initiated this seduction in the first place.

The rough denim of his jeans and the soft cotton of his T-shirt pressed against her naked flesh. How was he fully clothed? He had her at his mercy, when she'd planned to have him at hers.

Her legs began to shake and tremble. His thrusting fingers had begun to probe and stroke. Heat filled her belly as coils of tension tightened her muscles.

Clenching her jaw, she dug her fingernails into Ryan's shoulders. Her leg crept up farther and farther until she had it wrapped around his thigh.

Then he raised his head from her breast and pressed his warm lips against her mouth. As his tongue invaded her, she exploded.

Her other foot came off the floor, and only Ryan's body kept her upright as she thrust her hips against him over and over as the waves of her orgasm claimed her.

He kissed the sighs from her lips as she descended from paradise. When she once again had her feet firmly planted on the carpet, Ryan pinned her with his gaze and reached down to unbutton his fly.

His erection had been straining against his jeans, and once free, his hard, tight flesh brushed her belly.

He placed a hand on her shoulder, nudging her down.

She dropped to her knees in front of him. He was still fully clothed except for his jeans and the underwear twisted around his muscular thighs, exposing his throbbing erection.

She trailed her fingernails up the insides of his thighs, and his big body shivered. She took him gently into her mouth and he groaned, plowing his fingers through her hair.

He said through clenched teeth, "I don't think this is going to last very long."

She answered by wrapping her arms around his hips and digging her nails into his muscular buttocks. The musky taste of him filled her mouth, and at this moment she wanted nothing more.

How did she think she could hold herself aloof from this man? Disengage herself from the hot passion that coursed between them? Maybe she'd been fooling herself. Maybe she always knew how it would end between them.

And this had to be the end. Once he learned her true identity and her true purpose, he'd end it himself.

Oh, but right now it felt like a beginning.

He growled, a deep, animalistic sound from the back of his throat, and tugged on her hair, urging her to stand.

He kissed the pulse throbbing in her lower lip while he nudged his knee between her legs. Her heart galloped, skipping several beats along the way when she realized he planned to take her right here against the wall.

"There's a bed in this room, you know."

"We don't need a bed." He nipped her earlobe, and she sighed.

He forced her legs apart and slid one hand between her thighs. She hitched a leg around his waist, and he drove into her, pinning her against the wall.

She didn't know how or when she'd managed to hook the other leg around his waist, but nothing was holding her up except him.

Wrapped around his body, she glanced over his shoulder into the mirrored closet door across from them and gasped. She resembled some wild creature, naked limbs wrapped around Ryan's body, appearing to be a part of him, belonging to him.

Then she squeezed her eyes closed as her core tightened. His thrusts grew deeper and faster until the pressure finally broke and she cried out with her release.

She melted around him as the sweet pleasure continued to soak into her skin. He had to support her thighs with his splayed hands as she continued to straddle him.

Then his body stiffened, and his muscles tightened beneath her hands. The force of his passion exploded within her, and he moaned her name over and over as he spent himself inside her.

She'd never heard a sweeter sound.

At last he buried his face in the curve of her neck as they both panted. "That was even better than I imagined it would be."

Her legs slid down his thighs, and she grabbed on to his shoulders. "And when exactly did you start imagining this?"

A slow grin spread across his face, and he pinched her chin. "From the moment I carried you from that sauna."

Her pulse quickened. "You didn't know anything about me."

He snorted. "That's never stopped a man from fantasizing."

"You're still dressed." Her hands slid down to the front of his sweat-soaked T-shirt and she plucked it from his chest. "How is that even fair?"

"It's more than fair." Taking a step back, he hitched up his jeans, and his gaze tracked down her nude body, leaving prickles of heat in its wake. Then he swept her up in his arms as if she weighed no more than a kitten and carried her to the primly made bed.

He dropped her. "Now, let me get a good look at you."

"Isn't that what you were doing before?" Warmth swept across her body and she crossed her legs. "And when do I get my turn?"

He pulled off his heavy motorcycle boots and dropped them one at a time on the floor. Straddling her, he pulled his T-shirt over his head, revealing an expanse of rippling muscles.

"That's more like it." She reached out her hands toward the ridges on his chest and traced one hard line with her fingertip.

He twitched beneath her gentle touch. "I'm not done with you yet."

She couldn't help herself. When he talked like that and his bottle-green eyes roamed over her body, she turned to clay, only too happy to allow him to mold and shape her to his pleasure…and hers.

She moaned, and he chuckled. "You'd better hang on because I'm just getting started."

She'd worry about the plan later.

KACIE WOKE WITH a start and squinted at the green numbers floating in the pitch dark. Ryan's slow, steady breathing stirred the ends of her hair, and his leg hitched over her hip pinned her to his body.

And what a body. She'd finally gotten her chance to do her own exploration, and the memory would be seared into her brain forever.

She squirmed away from him, and he didn't move a muscle. Before they'd drifted off to sleep, she'd scoped out the location of the box containing the case files organized by his brother's fiancée—a box she hadn't known existed until dinner. Now she swept her cell phone from the nightstand and aimed the little beam of light across the room and under the desk by the window. It didn't quite reach her target, but she knew the general location.

When she rolled off the bed, she shivered, but the room wasn't even cold. She shuffled her feet on the carpet as she quietly made her way to the box.

Holding the cell-phone light before her, she crouched next to the box and flicked off the lid. She dug into the first set of files and read the neat headings on the labels until she came to a thick folder bound by two rubber bands.

This had to be it. She peered at the label and nodded to herself. She snapped off the first band and then rolled off the other one.

She flipped open the file and began to thumb through the contents, inspecting each photo.

A light came to life across the room and she gasped, dropping the folder on the floor.

"What the hell are you doing?"

YOUR PARTICIPATION IS REQUESTED!

Dear Reader,

Since you are a lover of our books – we would like to get to know you!

Inside you will find a short Reader's Survey. Sharing your answers with us will help our editorial staff understand who you are and what activities you enjoy.

To thank you for your participation, we would like to send you 2 books and 2 gifts – **ABSOLUTELY FREE!**

Enjoy your gifts with our appreciation,

Pam Powers

SEE INSIDE FOR READER'S SURVEY

For Your Reading Pleasure...

FREE!

We'll send you 2 books and 2 gifts
ABSOLUTELY FREE
just for completing our Reader's Survey!

Visit us at:
www.ReaderService.com

YOUR READER'S SURVEY
"THANK YOU" FREE GIFTS INCLUDE:
- ▶ **2 FREE books**
- ▶ **2 lovely surprise gifts**

PLEASE FILL IN THE CIRCLES COMPLETELY TO RESPOND

1) What type of fiction books do you enjoy reading? (Check all that apply)
- ○ Suspense/Thrillers   ○ Action/Adventure   ○ Modern-day Romances
- ○ Historical Romance   ○ Humour   ○ Paranormal Romance

2) What attracted you most to the last fiction book you purchased on impulse?
- ○ The Title   ○ The Cover   ○ The Author   ○ The Story

3) What is usually the greatest influencer when you <u>plan</u> to buy a book?
- ○ Advertising   ○ Referral   ○ Book Review

4) How often do you access the internet?
- ○ Daily   ○ Weekly   ○ Monthly   ○ Rarely or never

5) How many NEW paperback fiction novels have you purchased in the past 3 months?
- ○ 0 - 2   ○ 3 - 6   ○ 7 or more

YES! I have completed the Reader's Survey. Please send me the 2 FREE books and 2 FREE gifts (gifts are worth about $10) for which I qualify. I understand that I am under no obligation to purchase any books, as explained on the back of this card.

❏ I prefer the regular-print edition   ❏ I prefer the larger-print edition
182/382 HDL GF94   199/399 HDL GF94

FIRST NAME	LAST NAME

ADDRESS

APT.#	CITY

STATE/PROV.	ZIP/POSTAL CODE

EMAIL

◈ HARLEQUIN™ READER SERVICE — Here's How It Works:

Accepting your 2 free Harlequin Intrigue® books and 2 free gifts (gifts valued at approximately $10.00) places you under no obligation to buy anything. You may keep the books and gifts and return the shipping statement marked "cancel." If you do not cancel, about a month later we'll send you 6 additional books and bill you just $4.74 each for the regular-print edition or $5.49 each for the larger-print edition in the U.S. or $5.24 each for the regular-print edition or $5.99 each for the larger-print edition in Canada. That is a savings of at least 13% off the cover price. It's quite a bargain! Shipping and handling is just 50¢ per book in the U.S. and 75¢ per book in Canada.* You may cancel at any time, but if you choose to continue, every month we'll send you 6 more books, which you may either purchase at the discount price or return to us and cancel your subscription. *Terms and prices subject to change without notice. Prices do not include applicable taxes. Sales tax applicable in N.Y. Canadian residents will be charged applicable taxes. Offer not valid in Quebec. Books received may not be as shown. All orders subject to credit approval. Credit or debit balances in a customer's account(s) may be offset by any other outstanding balance owed by or to the customer. Please allow 4 to 6 weeks for delivery. Offer available while quantities last.

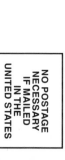

▲ If offer card is missing write to: Harlequin Reader Service, P.O. Box 1867, Buffalo, NY 14240-1867 or visit www.ReaderService.com ▲

BUSINESS REPLY MAIL
FIRST-CLASS MAIL   PERMIT NO. 717   BUFFALO, NY

POSTAGE WILL BE PAID BY ADDRESSEE

HARLEQUIN READER SERVICE
PO BOX 1867
BUFFALO NY 14240-9952

NO POSTAGE
NECESSARY
IF MAILED
IN THE
UNITED STATES

Chapter Nine

A pulse pounded against her temple, and she swallowed. "I—I had an idea and wanted to look up something."

Ryan's sleep-roughened voice rumbled across the room. "Are you kidding me? You're working?"

"Not exactly."

"Not at all. Get back to bed."

With trembling hands she gathered the scattered contents of the folder and hugged it to her chest. "Just a few more minutes. Go back to sleep. I'm sorry I woke you."

"I am, too, but now I am awake and I'll be damned if I'm gonna lie here while a naked woman is in my room working on the floor. Come on over here before I toss you over my shoulder and carry you back to bed. And don't think that wouldn't give me great pleasure…before I give you great pleasure."

The bed squeaked, and Kacie dumped the folder back into the box and tamped the lid back on it.

"No need to go caveman on me. I'm coming."

She extinguished her cell-phone light and stumbled back to the bed, where Ryan had flipped back the covers.

"Crawl in here, woman, and keep me warm." He patted the mattress.

She slid beneath the sheet, and Ryan pulled her back toward his chest, folding his warm body around hers.

He wrapped one arm around her, cupping her breast. "Brr. Seems like I need to warm *you* up. What possessed you to start working, stark naked, in the middle of the night?"

She yawned noisily and threaded her fingers through his. "I'll tell you in the morning."

BUT SHE DIDN'T tell him in the morning, and he didn't ask. Either he'd forgotten she ever left the warmth of their bed or he no longer deemed it important.

Fine with her.

She bit off the corner of her toast and waved it at his laptop on the breakfast table between them. "Anything important?"

"My assistant chief has everything under control. Most exciting thing I've missed is the town drunk falling off the wagon again and running his car into a ditch."

She dropped her toast and brushed the crumbs from her fingers. "Aah, small-town life. Is it enough for you?"

"Is it enough for *you?*" He clicked the keys of his keyboard without looking up. "You're outside of Seattle, right? Small town?"

"It suits me, but when I'm not spending my time writing and researching, I'm on the road. So, my small town is an oasis for me."

"Crestview is an oasis for me, too."

"An oasis from what?"

He tapped his head. "From the stuff going on up here."

"You seem well-adjusted to me." She tilted her head and tossed her hair over her shoulder. "All red-blooded American male."

"You got that right." He reached around his laptop and brushed a knuckle across her cheek. "But I've worked hard to reach this level of calm and serenity, and living in

Crestview helps. I work, I surf and I run the trails, and I have a tight-knit group of friends in town."

"And you have your brothers."

He choked on the sip of coffee he'd just taken. "I wouldn't exactly say hanging out with my brothers keeps me sane, but I think we've all worked through our issues in our different ways. This book and proving Dad's innocence once and for all will go a long way toward sealing the deal for all of us."

He took her hand and traced the pad of his thumb along the grooves of her knuckles. "Thanks to you."

"Save your thanks." She slid her hand from beneath his warm touch. He wouldn't be thanking her if he knew about her deception. Last night had changed so much between them, had changed her, but it couldn't alter her mission. She owed this to her mother. She had to see it through, regardless of her feelings for Ryan. Mom deserved justice even if her daughter had to make sacrifices. "I haven't done anything yet."

"You will. Any woman who gets up in the middle of the night to work after a couple of hours of passionate sex is going to get the job done."

She dropped her lashes and crumpled her napkin into a tight ball.

"What *were* you doing last night?" His gaze had returned to his laptop monitor, but his words seemed to hover over the table like an accusation.

"I was just wondering if Christina had anything in her notes about Cookie's previous encounter with your father."

His eyes flicked to her face and dropped again as she eased out a long, slow breath. "Did you find what you were looking for?"

"You rudely interrupted me and threatened to forcibly remove me from the floor. Remember?"

"Oh yeah. I would've had a lot of fun doing it, too." He wiggled his eyebrows up and down. "Cookie's having another open house this afternoon. I think we should pay her a surprise visit."

"Do you think it will do any good?"

"She's had some time to think about the past. Maybe she'll remember how my father helped her and decide to tell me the truth."

"If she hasn't already." She hunched over the table, clasping her hands in front of her, happy to change the subject. "Her nervousness might've just been coming from the fact that you brought up unpleasant memories from her past."

"Could be—" he tapped the screen "—but I have a sudden desire to see another house in the Sunset District, and maybe she'll put out more chocolate-chip cookies."

"What time?"

"Two to five. I figure we'll drop by closer to five to catch her alone."

"That'll work for me."

"Do you have plans?"

"I'm going to edit what I have so far as an introduction, so I'll be holed up in my room all afternoon."

"That'll give me time to do some work, too." He snapped his computer shut. "We can meet up again around four?"

"What kind of work?" She gripped the edge of the table. Maybe she should suggest they work side by side just so she could make sure he wasn't going through that box on his own.

His wide shoulders rose and fell. "Seems my assistant chief isn't that good after all. He wants me to look at a couple of reports and respond to a proposal from a new caterer trying to get a contract for our jail food."

"You have to deal with caterers as the chief of police?

Who knew?" She lifted one eyebrow and retrieved her purse from the back of her chair. As long as he didn't plan to go rummaging through that box—at least not until she got a crack at it first.

When the check came, Ryan let her pick it up this time to make her happy. She'd been on edge all morning. Did she regret the antics of the previous night?

He didn't.

Maybe it wasn't the smartest idea to bed the woman who was writing a book about your family, but she'd started it. He hadn't planned on taking her against the wall like that— or any other way—but she'd come on to him the previous night, no doubt about it.

He had no intention of turning down a lady like Kacie Manning. Was she regretting it now because he hadn't measured up in some way?

He pulled out her chair and she smiled her thanks as her gaze roamed hungrily over his body.

Hell no. He'd measured up in every way that mattered. But maybe she preferred her lovemaking slow and easy— nice and proper.

His eyes followed the sway of her hips as she wove through the tables of the restaurant.

Hell no. There was nothing proper about the way that woman liked to make love.

They were made for each other. They fit together like tongue and groove. Literally.

She made a sudden stop as she exited the restaurant and he stumbled against her.

"Sorry." He put a hand on her waist.

She shifted away from him and grabbed a newspaper from a rack. "My fault. I wanted one of these."

Definitely skittish.

She waved the paper at him. "Spencer Breck died."

"The billionaire who owns half the city?"

"Is there another Spencer Breck?" She studied the newsprint and whistled. "He's leaving one big estate."

"I know his wife died a few years ago, but he has kids. I'm sure he'll leave a lot to charity, too. Nobody can spend that much money."

"He has one child—London Breck—beautiful, skinny and now wealthy beyond belief." She tucked the newspaper into her bag.

"Poor girl." He punched the elevator button.

"You're kidding, right? She has everything."

Shrugging, he said, "All that money is nothing but trouble, and now there's going to be a lot of publicity because her father just died. Publicity is never good."

"Don't cry for London. That girl loves publicity—skinny-dipping in fountains, driving race cars, following rock bands."

"I guess some of us don't follow the gossip rags as much as others, so maybe it's not 'poor girl.' She sounds like a pain in the ass."

This time when the elevator reached her floor, she left him with a wave of her hand.

When he reached his room, he blew out a breath and shouldered open his door, letting it slam behind him. He pressed the palm of his hand against the wall where he'd pinned Kacie the night before and closed his eyes. He could almost detect her scent—sweet, musky and all woman.

He brushed his teeth and set up his laptop on the table by the window, kicking the cardboard box out of his way. The files within shifted and his gaze darted toward the box.

Maybe Kacie had been onto something last night. Had Christina made note of the fact that the only witness to his father's jump off the bridge knew him?

He lifted the lid from the box with the toe of his shoe

and pulled out the disheveled folder on top. The word on the label jumped at him: *Victims*.

In the dark, Kacie had grabbed the wrong file anyway. Any mention of Cookie wouldn't be in the file about the Phone Book Killer's victims.

He dropped that file to the floor and shuffled through the box. Christina hadn't created a separate file for the suicide. So maybe she hadn't made the same discovery about Cookie as he and Kacie had. Even more reason to talk to Cookie that afternoon.

He secured the lid back on the box and delved into Crestview police work.

Ryan worked through lunch since he and Kacie had gotten a late start that morning. He took a trip down the hallway and got a can of soda and a bag of chips from the vending machine.

As he popped the tab on the can, his gaze strayed to the box again. Christina had been so thorough about researching his dad's case, so thorough it had almost cost her the relationship with Eric. How had she missed that detail?

He swept his phone from the table and tapped on Christina's name in his address book.

She picked up after the first ring. "Hi, Ryan."

"Hey, Christina. Where are you?"

"I'm in D.C. with your brother. Is that why you called?"

That was Christina—all business. "No, I have a question about your research into Dad's case."

"How's the book coming? Have you met Kacie Manning yet?"

"I've met her and I have no idea how the book is coming. That's her business."

"Except you're calling me." She covered the phone and shouted an order to someone.

"Are you busy?"

"Not too busy to talk to one of my future brothers-in-law. What do you need to know?"

"Did you look into the woman who witnessed Dad's jump from the bridge?"

"Cookie Phelps, a hooker."

"Did you talk to her? Look her up?"

She cleared her throat. "No. I just got her name and statement from the case file on the murders."

"You never looked at the file on the suicide?"

"There was no file on the suicide."

"Sure there was…is. I picked it up from Records."

"That's weird. I never saw that file and nobody ever offered it to me."

"Well, I got it, and you wanna hear weird? My dad had arrested Cookie's pimp several years before Cookie witnessed his suicide."

Christina whistled. "That's a coincidence."

"Yeah, I guess so."

"You think there's some significance to it?"

"I met Cookie yesterday, and she was really nervous."

"Is she still in the life?"

"She's a Realtor."

"Makes sense she'd be jumpy about reminders from the past."

"Yeah, that's what Kacie figured."

"How is that intrepid true-crime writer, Ms. Manning? She must have some cojones to go toe-to-toe with that psychopath Daniel Walker."

"Umm, yeah." He took a sip of his drink, scrambling for a new subject or a way to end the call.

"Well, does she?"

Too late. He never should've taken a sip of soda. Christina was like a pit bull when she got hold of something. "Does she what?"

She sighed noisily. "Have cojones?"

"Not that I noticed."

Christina swore. "You're sleeping with her."

No wonder she was such a good FBI agent. His brother was in big trouble. "Because I didn't notice her cojones?"

She snorted. "Whatever. Keep us posted on what you dig up. And, Ryan?"

"Yeah?" He held his breath.

"Keep it in your pants."

He ended the call and shoved his phone across the table. Eric had told him that Christina was from a family of powerful *brujos,* and now he didn't doubt that at all.

He tapped his toe against the box. But not powerful enough to have gotten the suicide file.

He glanced at the clock on his computer and shoved it away from him. He had just enough time to go for a quick workout in the hotel gym, shower and change.

Maybe Kacie would agree to have dinner with him after they saw Cookie. The evening might not end up the same way it did the night before, but if Kacie wanted to dial back the passion and put him firmly in the friend zone, he'd comply like a gentleman.

That didn't mean he'd ever forget the previous night—the way she tasted, the way her smooth skin felt beneath his fingertips, the way she clung to him and took all he had to offer.

Better make that a cold shower.

KACIE STEPPED FROM the shower and pulled on a lacy thong and a matching bra—not that she planned on any high jinks with Ryan that night, but a girl never knew when she'd be in an accident and need to have her clothes sliced from her body. Best to be prepared.

Of course, if she did seduce Ryan again, she could place

herself back in his room in the dead of night and take another crack at the file in the box. All she needed was one picture.

And really, there wasn't much involved in the seduction of Ryan Brody. He wanted her—and she wanted him. That fact soothed her conscience. There was no trickery involved, at least during the seduction phase.

She studied her body in the mirror, naked except for the bit of froth between her legs. She cupped her breasts and ran her thumb across the reddish flesh where Ryan's beard had scuffed her. Closing her eyes, she sank against the vanity. She could make the sacrifice one more night to get her hands on that picture.

The knock on the door made her jump and her eyes flew open. She stuffed herself into the bra and tiptoed to the door. Pressing her eye to the peephole, she called out. "One minute, Brody."

She wriggled into a pair of skinny jeans and snagged a black camisole from the dresser drawer.

Panting slightly, she pulled open the door to her hotel room. "Are you early again?"

"Right on time." He tapped his watch. "Were you working or daydreaming?"

A little of both.

"All work and no play. I think I got a good start on the intro to the book."

She'd flung open the door and Ryan had stood with his shoulder wedged against the wall as she grabbed a blouse from the closet and shoved her feet into a pair of flats.

"Can I read it?"

She scurried to her laptop and made a few quick clicks with the mouse. "Not yet."

Not until I have another opportunity to savor every inch of your delicious body before you discover my true intent.

He threw up his hands. "Okay. Am I going to have to read it along with everyone else?"

"I think that's a good idea." She leaned close to the mirror and spread some lip gloss across her lips with the tip of her little finger.

"Just like Walker."

She dropped the tube of gloss. "What?"

"He didn't read the book until it was published, either, did he?"

"Nope. Do you want to get some dinner after we see Cookie?"

"Sure." His green eyes lit up, almost as though they were shooting sparks.

Oh yeah. Getting Brody back into bed tonight would be easy.

Ryan drove to the open house in his car, since parking on the residential streets of the Sunset District was easier and faster than taking public transportation. They pulled up to the curb across the street from the house, and Ryan pointed to the blue sedan parked in front. "That's her car, but I don't see any others. You think she's alone?"

"If she's not, we can pretend to be interested buyers until the real interested buyers leave."

They slid from the car, both of them snapping their doors shut as if fearing Cookie would hear them out there and take flight.

Kacie approached the slightly ajar door first and placed the palm of her hand against the green-painted wood. She eased it open and stepped into the house.

The smell of freshly baked cookies had her mouth

watering, and she winked at Ryan. "You're in luck. You can probably have all the leftover cookies."

He didn't return her smile. Instead, his gaze darted around the room as his jaw tensed.

His concern radiated out toward her. She scanned the empty living room and kitchen, her brow furrowing. "Do you think she saw us coming?"

Putting his finger to his lips, he shook his head.

Did that mean he didn't think she saw them coming or that he wanted her to keep quiet? And why?

Ryan poked his head into the kitchen. "Look at the cookies."

Mounds of dough crowded a cookie sheet, while the oven clicked and heated up the room.

"Looks like she left in a hurry." Kacie turned off the oven and backpedaled out of the kitchen. "Or maybe she's in the backyard with some potential buyers."

A side door led from the kitchen to a small patio. Ryan jiggled the handle and then opened the door. He shuffled onto the brick patio, and Kacie crossed the room to peer down the short hallway.

Maybe Cookie was in the bathroom.

"Cynthia?" Kacie took two steps down the carpeted hallway and froze. She tilted her head. Was that a noise? Was Cookie hiding from them back there?

"Cynthia, we just want to talk to you." Trailing her hand along the wall, Kacie took several more steps down the hall.

The door of the first room stood open, and she glanced inside. A lone wicker wastebasket gaped at her from its side in the center of the room.

She continued to the next open door and ducked her head inside. She stumbled backward, clutching her throat.

The room was empty…except for Cookie's bloodied and crumpled body in the corner.

Chapter Ten

She must've screamed.

"What is it?" Ryan bumped her shoulder as he crowded past her into the room. He swore and strode across the carpet, dropping to the floor next to Cookie's body.

"What happened to her?" Kacie felt like such a chicken, but she stayed back, clinging to the doorjamb.

"Call 911. She's still breathing."

Kacie twirled around to retrieve the purse she'd left on the kitchen counter. Now she really felt like a coward. The woman was alive and suffering, and all she could do was scream like a ninny.

She dumped the contents of her purse onto the counter and grabbed her cell phone. She babbled over the phone until the operator asked her for the address.

She knew the street name and stumbled outside to read the number from the front of the house.

Clutching her phone between clammy hands, she returned to the bedroom. Ryan had found a towel and was wrapping it around Cookie's head, stanching the flow of her blood.

"An ambulance is on the way. What happened to her? Is she going to be okay?"

"Someone beat her to a pulp." Ryan tucked in the ends of the towel to secure it and picked up Cookie's wrist to feel for a pulse. "As to whether or not she's going to be okay, I have no idea. She's in bad shape."

Kacie's stomach churned and she sealed one hand over her mouth.

Sirens wailed, and Ryan glanced up. "Go out front and meet them."

Grateful to have something useful to do, Kacie rushed from the room and tripped onto the porch. The ambulance came to a screeching halt behind Cookie's car, with two cop cars hot on its heels.

As she led the EMTs to Cookie's inert form, she told them as much as she knew. They got to work immediately as Ryan backed up, giving them space.

He held out his hands, stained with Cookie's blood.

"Did she say anything, Ryan? Was she conscious?"

"No."

The presence of the police officers halted any conversation between her and Ryan. She'd wondered how much of the truth Ryan was prepared to give to the cops, but she should've known better. He told them everything. Of course, they'd have probably figured out sooner or later that Ryan Brody, the police chief of Crestview, wasn't house shopping in the city.

Before their conversation with the police ended, the EMTs wheeled Cookie from the house.

"Wait—her purse." Kacie grabbed Cookie's purse from the counter, and her phone slid out. Her eyes shifted to the side, where Ryan was still talking to the cops, and then she snatched the phone and slid it into her back pocket.

Not everyone was as honest as Ryan Brody.

She dangled the purse from its handle. "Should this go with her to the hospital?"

"We'll take that, ma'am." One of the cops held out his hand and she hung the purse over his arm.

The police kept them for another fifteen minutes before releasing them, although the work of law enforcement had just begun. She and Ryan crossed paths with a horde of crime-scene investigators and additional cops and detectives.

When they got to the car, Ryan rested his hands on the steering wheel and blew out a breath. "Wow."

"What are you thinking, Brody?"

He turned his head and his jaw relaxed for the first time since they had entered the open house. "Are you all right? You were as pale as a ghost in there."

"I'm fine. You'd think I'd be used to it by now—two violent-crime victims in the space of a few days."

"That's right." He drummed his thumbs against the steering wheel.

"What do you think happened?"

"Someone came to the open house and beat her."

"I know that, but why?"

"Why do you think?"

She swallowed and ran her tongue across her dry teeth. "Because of us? Because she talked to us?"

He drove the heels of his hands against the steering wheel. "It seems that way, doesn't it?"

"Why?"

"Someone doesn't want her talking to us."

"Do you think," she said, licking her lips, "that whoever beat her up wanted her dead?"

"I don't think he cared one way or the other. Even if she doesn't die, she's not going to talk now. She got the message—loud and clear."

She gripped his forearm, her nails digging into his corded muscle. "What's going on, Ryan? Why would someone want to keep Cookie quiet? She witnessed your father's suicide. That's public record."

"She must know more." He smacked his thigh. "She knows something, or someone thinks she does. We had our opportunity to find out yesterday. We had the element of surprise, and we blew it."

"*She* blew it. She should've told us everything she knew yesterday. If she was scared or worried, maybe you could've given her some protection, or the SFPD could've helped."

"She was obviously scared. I should've pressed her."

"Shoulda, coulda, woulda. We didn't and she didn't, and now we just have to figure out who attacked her and why."

He jerked his thumb over his shoulder. "I'm hoping the cops can come up with some evidence—if we didn't destroy it all by traipsing through the house."

"I believe in being proactive." She patted her purse, where she'd slipped Cookie's phone. "If I had to count only on law enforcement in writing my book about Walker, I never would've had a book."

"What do you mean?" He raised an eyebrow at her.

She dug into her handbag and pulled out Cookie's phone. "I have this."

"Congratulations. You have a phone."

"Not just any phone." She tilted it back and forth. "Cookie's phone."

This time his eyebrows jumped to his hairline. "You stole a piece of evidence from a crime scene?"

"I don't see it that way. Cookie's murder is directly related to us, and we deserve to take a few matters into our own hands instead of relying on the SFPD to feed us info when and if they want to."

He shook his head. "You have a loose concept of ethics."

Heat flashed in her cheeks and she turned to her open window to gulp in a few breaths of fresh air. He didn't know the half of it. "Do you want to see Cookie's incoming and outgoing calls or don't you?"

His gaze strayed past her and took in the law-enforcement personnel scurrying in and out of the open house. "Not here."

He put the car in gear and pulled away from the curb. He cruised around the neighborhood and then stopped in front of a park. Punching on the dome light, he said, "Let's do this."

Kacie tapped Cookie's smartphone to wake it up. "Let's see. First, I guess we can see any recent calls."

She brought the phone beneath the light, and Ryan leaned in, his head touching hers. She ran her finger down five calls. "She doesn't get many calls for a Realtor, or else she deletes them."

"These three have names attached, so I'm assuming they're family or friends, but these two are listed as being blocked—one last night, one this morning."

She tapped on one blocked call but nothing happened. "I guess you can't call back a blocked number."

"What about any texts?"

She accessed Cookie's messages. "Ah, more prolific here, but it looks like they're mostly work-related—back and forths about properties, financing, open houses."

"Any messages about today's open house? Her assailant could've been posing as a house hunter. In fact, that's the most likely scenario."

"Here's a thread about it." She read the messages aloud to Ryan. "So, someone just double-checking the time and square footage of the lot."

"Is there a name associated with those texts?"

"No, but there's a phone number."

"How about—" he took the phone from her "—we send this person a text, posing as Cookie?"

"Go ahead."

He read his message as he entered it. "'Still interested in the house on Gladys? CP.'"

Kacie held her breath as Ryan cupped the phone in the palm of his hand. They both focused on the hypnotic blinking cursor for a good two minutes before Kacie released her breath.

"I guess he's not going to respond right away."

"Or ever. If this is our guy, he's gotta figure the police have his phone and are doing a little research."

She sat back and tilted her head against the headrest. "He's also gotta figure the police can trace that number, right? You *can* trace that number, can't you?"

"I can pull some strings and get a line on that number, sure."

"That's a start. What about those two blocked numbers?"

"I'll work on it."

Kacie covered her face with her hands and massaged her temples. "I don't get it. Why would someone want to harm Cookie?"

"Why would someone want to harm Dr. Franklin, my father's police therapist?"

"What are you talking about?" She peered at him through her fingers.

"When my brother Sean decided to question Dr. Franklin, he wound up having a heart attack. I approach Cookie Phelps, and she winds up in a coma. Someone doesn't want my father's case reopened."

"And the only reason for that is that someone doesn't want the truth to come out."

"The truth is he didn't do it."

She held up her hands. "Whoa. That was a big leap."

"Was it?" He cocked his head, his eyes narrowing. "The current story is that my father was the Phone Book Killer and then offed himself to avoid detection and prosecution. If that were the truth, why bother harming all these people twenty years later if all they were going to do was confirm that truth?"

"It could be the other way around." She folded her hands in her lap and stared at her white knuckles. "What if Dr. Franklin and Cookie had some irrefutable proof that your father *was* the Phone Book Killer, and someone wants to suppress that? After all, nobody ever proved that he was."

The silence from the other side of the car seemed to drag on forever. Kacie turned her head to take in Ryan's profile, which seemed carved from granite.

He spoke, barely moving his lips. "That makes no sense."

"I guess not. I'm just trying to look at all angles here." She nibbled on her lower lip and stared out the window. His supposition made more sense than hers, but what did that mean for her? What did it mean for the book? And more important, had she just revealed her hand to Ryan?

The chill from his side of the car almost had her reaching for her jacket.

He cranked on the engine. "I'm going to look into this phone number."

"After dinner?"

"Dinner?" He turned a pair of icy green eyes on her. "You really have an appetite after discovering Cookie?"

She swallowed past the lump in her throat as tears stung the backs of her eyes. *Idiot.* She'd leaked her personal agenda, and now that Ryan had gotten a glimpse of it, he no longer trusted her.

To be fair, she no longer trusted herself. Not where Ryan was concerned.

She knew the Brody brothers believed fervently in their father's innocence. They'd shut out anyone who challenged that belief.

And the irony of the situation was that she didn't even

know if she had an agenda anymore. She didn't know what to believe about Joseph Brody.

All she knew now was that she'd just lost the trust of a man she'd been falling for—a man she was having a hard time figuring out how to live without.

But she wasn't about to give up. Hadn't she always fought for what she wanted? With two beautiful older sisters, the biological daughters of her adoptive parents, she'd always felt as if she had to assert herself. She knew now that the struggle had been all in her head. Her parents hadn't really loved her any less than they had Fiona and Calista, but she'd always tried to get them to love her more because she had always felt less worthy.

She wasn't going to stand by and allow this amazing man to slip through her fingers. It was time to switch gears.

She put her hand over his. "I'm sorry. I'm sorry I doubted your father. Of course your theory makes much more sense than mine."

His arm tensed and then he turned off the car. "You don't have to apologize for doing your job. If we're going to get at the truth, we should discuss every angle, however sordid, however painful. Judd and I used to roll our eyes at Sean and Eric and how fierce they were in defense of Dad. Now I've gotten the same way. I've allowed myself to get sucked into this blood-is-thicker-than-water mentality where family can do no wrong."

"It's understandable, Ryan. If someone were making horrible claims about a member of my family, I'd probably defend that family member to the death."

He slipped his hand from beneath hers and squeezed her thigh. "But you're not just someone, and you're not making horrible claims. You're playing devil's advocate. I get it. You're doing your job, and I acted like an ass."

She put two fingers to his lips. "I totally get it, but I

didn't want to let your anger fester. I don't want any mis-understandings between us."

He puckered his lips and kissed her fingers. "Usually I'm the same way, but I admit it. This case has gotten under my skin, and now I feel responsible for Cookie's predicament."

"How were we supposed to know she'd pay for talking to us?"

"Dr. Franklin paid, too."

"We don't even know that." Her stomach growled and she pressed a hand to it. "Would you really consider me a horrible person if I wanted to get something to eat? It doesn't have to be five-star or anything."

He chuckled and squeezed her thigh a little higher, which caused a slow flush to fan out across her skin. "I channeled Sean there for a minute. He's great at guilting people, too. I'm sorry about Cookie, but I'm also starving."

She slumped in her seat. "I'm so glad to hear you say that. Literally, I could eat anything."

"Tacos from a hole-in-the-wall stand?"

"Lead the way."

He revved up the car again and peeled away from the curb.

Twenty minutes later, they pulled into the crowded parking lot of a taco stand in South San Francisco. The lines at the windows curled around the parking lot.

"Looks like we're not the only ones who need a quick fix." She reached into the backseat for her jacket as Ryan pulled his car around the back of the building and parked it on some dirt.

They shuffled to the back of the line, and Kacie plucked Cookie's phone from her purse. "Are we going to try calling the number from the open-house texts?"

"Yeah, just not from our phones or the hotel."

"I guess we can try to find a pay phone."

"There are still a few of those left." He nudged her to keep up with the line. "Let's eat first and call later."

They each ordered a couple of tacos and Ryan added a burrito to his order. He paid in cash, and then they stood to the side of the window, waiting for their number to be called.

He tugged on the ends of her hair. "Grab that table over there, and I'll wait for our order."

She threaded her way through the lines at the windows and scooted onto a picnic bench next to a family of four.

Ryan had accepted her apology and had even called her forthright. She rubbed her twitching eye. She had to tell him the truth. He'd be angry at first, but then he'd appreciate her honesty. Wouldn't he?

There was no reason to keep the truth from him anymore. The book she'd planned to write had taken a detour. The same thing had happened with the Walker book. When would she learn about preconceived notions?

Of course, if she never revealed the truth to Ryan, he'd never know that she'd come into this project with an agenda. But if they ever ended up together, she'd have to tell him. She couldn't keep such a big secret from him.

She glanced up and spotted him carrying a box of food overflowing with chips. Could they really end up together? Did they have a chance?

He placed the box on the table. "I asked for extra chips and salsa, but I think they went overboard."

She dipped a chip into the salsa and held it up. "You can never have too much chips and salsa."

"Watch it. That stuff's hot." He straddled the bench across from her.

She bit into the chip with a crunch and the salsa dribbled down her chin. Before she had a chance to grab a napkin from the dispenser, he dabbed her chin with his thumb. "You're supposed to eat it, not wear it."

She chewed and swallowed, the salsa burning the roof of her mouth. "Thanks for that bit of advice."

They both dug into their food, and cheap tacos on the street had never tasted so good. For the duration of the meal, she forgot about Cookie and Daniel Walker and even Joseph Brody. For the duration of the meal, they were two people with an undeniable attraction for each other out on a simple date.

But the meal ended.

"I think I saw a pay phone across the street at the gas station." He crumpled the wrapper from his last taco and tossed it into the box. "You game?"

"Absolutely." She patted her face with a napkin. "No more salsa on my face?"

He wedged a finger beneath her chin and tilted her head back. "Your face looks perfect."

Oh no, she wasn't ready to give up any part of that.

They relinquished their coveted seats to another couple hovering nearby and shoved their trash into the garbage can.

The light changed and they dashed across the street to the service station. Ryan grabbed her hand and tugged. "I think it's on the side of the mini-mart. I saw it when we were driving up the street."

They turned the corner of the squat building that housed a small convenience store. A light glowed over the pay phone.

Ryan picked up the receiver.

"Does it work?"

"We'll soon see." He dropped a coin in the slot and snapped his fingers for the number on Cookie's phone.

Kacie brought up the text and read the number aloud to him.

He punched it in and listened, while she pinched his shirtsleeve. "Well?"

He slammed the phone back in the cradle. "No answer and no voice mail."

"That in itself tells me something." She shoved Cookie's phone back in her purse. "Who doesn't have some kind of message on their phone, especially if you're using that phone to look for a house?"

"I don't know. Maybe he only responds to texts."

"Well, he didn't respond to our text, either."

"I didn't expect much, Kacie. I'm still going to try to trace the blocked phone calls. I can call the station tonight and get one of my guys on it." He rubbed a circle on her back and it almost soothed away her disappointment.

She combed her fingers through her hair and clasped it into a ponytail. "I suppose if someone had answered the phone and confirmed he or she was a valid house hunter, it would've been a dead end. This at least leaves us an opening."

They jogged back across the street and squeezed between the cars in the parking lot to get to Ryan's SUV in the dirt.

"At least we didn't get towed."

"No ticket?" She peeked at the windshield. "Looks like you got away with your illegal parking job, Brody. Did you put some kind of cop vibe around the car?"

"Yeah, it's a secret shield."

He opened the door for her and she slid onto the seat, closing her eyes.

The car jostled as Ryan climbed into the driver's side. "Are you okay?"

"It's been a long day. Not what I expected. Can we call the hospital and check on Cookie?"

"Sure." He pulled out his own phone and called information for San Francisco General. The operator must've automatically connected him because he began speaking.

"I'm calling to find out about a patient who was brought in earlier by ambulance, Cynthia Phelps." He tapped her knee and shook his head. "This is Chief Ryan Brody from Crestview. I'm the one who found her. You can check with the SFPD."

He recited his phone number and dropped the phone in his cup holder. "They wouldn't give me any info, but she's going to check with the P.D. and call me back if they give the go-ahead."

"Sheesh, you can't even check on anyone's welfare anymore without a full-scale investigation?"

"Don't worry. I'll get the news one way or another."

He pulled out of the parking lot, his tires stirring up dirt and rocks on the way out. He merged onto the freeway back to the city and their hotel.

The hypnotic headlights and her full tummy had Kacie's eyelids drooping. If she hoped for a repeat of the night before, she'd better get a boost of adrenaline from somewhere.

Maybe just getting a glimpse of Ryan's hard body would be enough to jump-start her libido.

The car bounced as Ryan left the freeway and turned onto the Embarcadero. He made another turn and the tires squealed as Kacie's head bumped the window.

"Hey!" Her eyelids flew open. "What do you think this is, the Indy 500?"

Ryan clutched the steering wheel. "This car isn't behaving too well."

"Maybe if you'd spring for a newer model, Brody."

The traffic light ahead glowed yellow and the car

lurched and then flew through the intersection as the light turned to red.

She gripped the edge of her seat. "Wow, Brody, just because you're a cop doesn't mean you can get away with murder in this city."

She clapped a hand over her mouth. Bad choice of words. But before she had time to apologize, the car sailed through another intersection, narrowly missing two pedestrians.

"Brody! What the hell are you doing?"

"It's the brakes." He hunched forward over the steering wheel. "We don't have any."

Chapter Eleven

He stomped on the brake pedal again, but the car surged forward. Aiming for the side of the road, he reached for the emergency brake. He yanked it up and the car lurched and growled.

It didn't stop, but it did slow down.

Kacie gasped beside him. "Is it going to stop?"

"Not without a fight." He pumped the brake, and his foot hit the floor.

He rushed up on a car stopped at a crosswalk. He careened around it, blowing by the shocked faces of the pedestrians startled to a halt in the street.

He couldn't keep this up. The closer they got to the busy end of the wharf, the less space he'd have to maneuver in. He needed something to slow him down, some obstacle in his path.

"Make sure your seat belt's snug."

Kacie tugged on her belt. "What are you going to do?"

"Hang on."

The curb, a couple of benches…and barriers. His tires bumped the curb, and he aimed the car between two groups of people. His vehicle jumped when he hit the curb and plowed toward the first bench.

Kacie yelled something unintelligible.

They ripped through the bench to the sound of screaming metal. The car limped forward.

His body tensed as he made a beeline for the orange barriers stationed along the walkway. The car smacked the barrier, and the air bags exploded.

He grunted as the bag hit his chest. Kacie gave a muffled cry.

The car lurched back, finally at rest.

Ryan struggled out of the smashed car and ran to the passenger side. He didn't like the look of the black smoke curling up from the collapsed hood. He yanked open Kacie's door and helped her from her position pinned between the air bag and the seat of the car.

They both staggered away from the wreckage as alternating sirens filled the air.

"Are you hurt?" He turned Kacie to face him and touched the abrasion on her cheek.

She held her hands in front of her. "I think I'm okay. You?"

"Tossed around, but nothing broken."

"You have some glass in your hair. Close your eyes." She flicked his hair with her fingers.

"Don't cut yourself."

She grabbed his T-shirt. "What just happened, Ryan?"

"Someone tampered with my brakes."

Her eyes widened, and then the EMTs and the cops descended.

The men in white checked his vitals and bandaged a small cut on his hand. The police weren't as solicitous. They'd gotten a few calls about his reckless driving before the crash and weren't altogether convinced he wasn't drunk or crazy.

"It was the brakes. They failed."

He still had to blow into the cop's face, but since he

showed no outward signs of drinking and the cop couldn't smell any alcohol on his breath, he didn't have to take a Breathalyzer.

Once he showed the officers his own badge and they realized he was Sean Brody's brother, he got the kid-glove treatment.

Kacie didn't have any severe injuries, but that red spot on her face from the air bag was going to turn into a nasty bruise.

"Were you having problems with your brakes before, Chief Brody?"

"You can call me Ryan, and no. I drove down here from Crestview and didn't have any issues with the brakes. Brakes were fine when we went to eat, and then it was sudden, like the lines were cut."

The officer raised his brows, but he wrote Ryan's suspicions in his notebook. "We'll have the car towed and our mechanic will check that. Anyone we need to question?"

Yeah, the same guy who'd beat up Cookie Phelps.

"I can't give you any names, but I'm almost positive this was no accident."

The cop took more information from Ryan and then offered to give them a lift to their hotel.

They made it back to the hotel and he didn't even have to ask Kacie to join him in his room. She collapsed on the bed, clutching the ice pack the EMTs had given her.

He pointed to the blue pack. "That's supposed to go on your face."

"When did he do it?"

He reached into his travel bag and pulled out a bottle, then popped a couple of ibuprofen in his mouth and chugged some water. "Must've done it while we were at the taco stand."

"That means…"

"Someone's been following us." He shook the bottle of gel caps at her. "I think you need a couple of these."

"No kidding." She held out her hands and he tossed her the bottle. "Maybe that's how he found out we met Cookie yesterday."

"Somebody knows we're working on Dad's case, and they want us to stop. Do you still think it's someone who wants us to preserve the commonly held belief that Dad was a serial killer?"

"I never said I believed that. I was just throwing out the possibility."

"Okay, I get it."

"Here's another possibility." She pressed the ice pack to her face and wrinkled her nose. "What if the brakes tonight don't have anything to do with Cookie or your father?"

He stopped pacing. "Really?"

"Think about it. Duke Bannister warned me about Walker. Someone locked me in the sauna, sent that doll and then killed Bannister. Maybe that's the person who tampered with your brakes. Maybe this is Walker's work."

"I think you've got it backward, Kacie." He rested his forehead against the cool glass of the window and watched a homeless man navigate his cart around a bus stop.

"What do you mean?"

"Maybe all of those previous incidents are connected to my father and this book. Maybe Walker was telling the truth for once in his life—he had nothing to do with the sauna or the doll or Bannister. After that interview you did on TV, plenty of people knew this was your next project."

She sat up and the ice pack fell to the floor. "You just rocked my reality. I never thought of that possibility before."

"I'm surprised. You're a good, insightful reporter. If you're in the business of looking at all possibilities, I'm shocked this one never occurred to you."

Hunching forward, she gathered the bedspread in her fists. "So, right from the beginning, before the two of us even met, someone was on my tail, harassing me, wanting me to believe Walker was after me. And all the time it was this book."

"That's what it's beginning to look like to me. This was never about Walker."

"Then Bannister was working for someone else." She bounced on the mattress, clapping her hands.

"That's what he wanted to tell you at the end. He was going to come clean about who sent him."

"He was murdered before he could do it."

"Just like Cookie was beaten before she could give us any more information."

"This is big, Brody, if it's true." This time she couldn't contain her excitement and she bounded from the bed. "We're onto something and maybe it starts with your father's suicide. Maybe he said something to Cookie before he jumped. Maybe he implicated someone else."

"And that someone else is alive and well in the city of San Francisco."

"Alive and well and targeting people who dare tell the truth or try to."

"There's just one problem." He crossed his arms and leaned against the window. "This is just a theory. We have no hard evidence to back it up, and we have no line on any suspects. We might as well be at square one."

"No, no." She shook her head and winced. "This is so much better than square one, Ryan. This is clarity. This is truth."

"This is supposition." Her reaction puzzled him. The pithy facts they had before them didn't warrant Kacie's level of excitement. Maybe she had a concussion. "Are you feeling okay?"

"A little sore. But more than ever I'm ready to tackle this project."

"I'm glad the car crash energized you, but you need to get some rest. We're both going to be feeling it tomorrow."

She folded her hands in front of her and dropped her lashes. "Can I stay with you tonight, Ryan? After everything that happened today, I'm feeling jittery. This person, whoever he is, must know we're staying in this hotel."

He crossed to the bed in two strides and gently enfolded her in his arms. He kissed the top of her head and the scrape on her face, which was already turning into a yellow bruise.

"Of course you're staying here tonight."

She held up one finger. "Give me a few minutes. I'm going to run to my room and brush my teeth and all that stuff."

"Do you want me to come with you?"

"I'll be okay. I promise not to get into the elevator with any strangers."

"I'll see you downstairs and wait outside your room just in case."

She kissed his mouth. "I knew you would."

Several minutes later back in her own room, Kacie changed into her pajamas. In the bathroom, she leaned toward the mirror and smoothed some night cream over the abrasion on her face.

She'd been so focused on her vendetta against the Brody family, she hadn't even considered there may be more to the story. Someone knew she was writing this book about Joey Brody and was trying to stop her from uncovering the truth—that Brody had been innocent.

That truth would smooth over everything between her and Ryan, giving them a clear path to some kind of relationship.

She just had one small detail to take care of first.

She wrapped the hotel robe around her body, grabbed

her purse and swung open the door to find Ryan propped up against the wall outside her room. "You didn't have to wait out here."

"No problem. Made me feel better to get a clear view of the hallway."

"All quiet?"

"Except for a couple too drunk to walk straight? Yeah."

She joined him in the hall and he escorted her back to his room. She hung her purse over the back of a chair and then stood in the center of the room, twisting her fingers in front of her.

Ryan turned on the radio and whipped the covers back from the bed. "My bed is yours."

She liked the sound of that. She shed her robe, crawled under the covers and fluffed up a pillow against the headboard.

He pulled off his T-shirt, and wearing a pair of boxers low on his hips, he slid into bed next to her.

Was she expected to keep her hands to herself with this prime male specimen sprawled out next to her?

He rolled to his side and slid his hands beneath her pajama top. As he cupped her breasts, he nuzzled her ear and whispered, "Do you always overdress for bed?"

Her nipples peaked beneath the rough pads of his fingertips and her insides melted.

"Do you?" She slid her hand along the waistband of his boxers and rolled them down to expose his readiness. He was already hard, his erection filling her hand.

He sucked in a breath and nipped her earlobe. "You've been manhandled enough today. I promise to take it nice and easy."

She sighed and yanked off her top. "You can take me any way you like."

His grin widened as he rolled on top of her and slid both

hands beneath her bottom, then moved down her body, taking her pajamas off along the way. "Let's start by releasing some of this tension."

He dipped his head between her legs, and she couldn't remember her own name, let alone the events of the day.

True to his word, they made love nice and easy, but every time he took her over the precipice she felt as if she'd died a thousand deaths.

Spent, they lay in each other's arms, their limbs tangled, their bodies joined with no beginning and no ending. The picture from the TV cast a flickering blue light across Ryan's strong face. How had she fallen so hard and so fast for this man?

She'd started this project placing Ryan Brody, all the Brody boys, in the role of the enemy. She couldn't help it. Even though the sons weren't guilty for the sins of the father, she'd put a black mark next to every Brody. But Ryan had torpedoed that role the very first night they'd met when he'd carried her from the sauna.

They'd do this together. They'd prove his father's innocence, perhaps find a measure of justice for her mother and write a kick-ass book in the process.

But first things first.

She picked up his heavy arm, which lay across her midsection, kissed the inside of his forearm and placed it across his chest.

He murmured and kicked one leg. She should wait until he was sound asleep, but then she'd be sound asleep, too.

She watched the reality show on TV for a few more minutes, listening to Ryan's steady breathing. She rolled away from him, and he tossed his head to the side.

She reached out and stroked the ridges of muscle that formed his chest. What a beautiful man—and he wanted her, thought she was beautiful and desirable. Made her feel beautiful and desirable for the first time in her life.

Her adoptive mom had always told her most men liked a woman with healthy curves, but it took Ryan Brody's unabashed lust for her body to finally make her believe it.

She kissed one of the brown nipples on his chest, her tongue flicking over the saltiness. He didn't move.

Releasing a breath, she rolled to the edge of the bed and swung her legs over the side. The bruised spot on her hip thudded with pain.

The glow from the TV cast enough light in the room that she could make it to the box by the window without tripping over anything. She knelt beside the box and tipped off the lid.

Her pulse quickened. The victim file was no longer on top, where she'd left it. Had Ryan been going through the files?

She dug in the box and found the file halfway down the stack. Glancing over her shoulder at Ryan's sleeping form, she pulled out the file and sat cross-legged on the floor with the folder in her lap.

She shuffled through the papers to get to each photo until she found the one she was looking for. She pulled the picture out of the stack and stuffed the file back into the box beneath the other folders.

With trembling fingers, she gripped the edges of the picture, her gaze sweeping the room. She couldn't very well go back to her room right now. If Ryan woke up while she was gone, she'd have way too much explaining to do. She'd have to hide it in this room and take it with her when she returned to her own room in the morning.

She considered and then rejected several options before deciding on her purse. She'd have to fold the picture, but she planned to shred it anyway.

She tiptoed to her handbag, still hanging on the back of the chair, and creased the photo in half before stuffing it into the depths of her purse.

She brushed her hands together. Ryan didn't ever have to know about that.

She crawled back into bed and snuggled against his warm body, running her hand up his muscular thigh before draping her leg over his.

This was going to work out. She'd make sure of it.

THE FOLLOWING MORNING, Kacie opened one eye and groaned.

Ryan looked up from the table by the window, fully dressed. "I think it's best if you hit the ibuprofen as soon as possible. I'm just beginning to be able to move my limbs without hissing in pain."

She smacked her lips and croaked. "Good idea."

"I put a couple of gel tabs and a glass of water on the nightstand for you."

"Thanks." She popped the pills and gulped down the water. "What are you working on so early?"

"I'm contacting my department to see if they can request a trace on that blocked phone number on Cookie's phone. It might lead to nothing, but then, that's why they're called leads."

"Glad someone's thinking clearly this morning."

He tapped some keys on the keyboard. "I need Cookie's number and the times of the calls. You still have her phone, right?"

"Uh-huh." She yawned.

"You put it in your purse before the accident last night."

Her heart slammed against her rib cage. "Yeah, it's still in my purse. I'll get it." She yelped as she scrambled to a sitting position.

"That's how I felt this morning. Let the meds take effect before you start moving around. I'll get the phone."

With her muscles screaming at her almost as loudly as the voice screaming in her head, Kacie clenched her teeth and sat up, flinging the covers from her body. "That's okay. I'll get it."

Too late. Ryan had her purse in his hands, spreading it open. "I'll find it."

"My purse is a mess. Toss it over here. I'll dump it out on the bed."

"I can do that here." Before she could say another word, he dumped the contents of her purse onto the table.

With wide eyes, she watched the folded photo drift to the floor. Maybe he'd leave it there.

He plucked Cookie's phone from the table. "Got it. That wasn't so bad."

He began to gather the rest of her items and shove them back into her purse.

"That's okay, Ryan. I'll do that."

"Sorry. Something fell on the floor." He crouched down and pinched the corner of the photo between two fingers.

Kacie held her breath, her heart pounding.

He couldn't have picked up the picture in a worse way. It flipped on its side as he dropped it onto the table, the stamp from the SFPD clearly visible.

He tapped Cookie's phone and Kacie's breath came back in short spurts. She eased from the bed. No sense in tempting fate. She had to get that photo back into her purse.

She made it halfway to the table when Ryan's gaze shifted from the phone's display to the photo on the table.

"What is this? It looks like a piece of evidence, a photo." He squinted at the stamp on the white background. "It's a photo of a victim."

Kacie reached out one hand. "I-it's…it's…"

Ryan unfolded the picture and smoothed it out on the table, his eyebrows colliding over his nose. "I know this picture."

Kacie crossed her arms over her belly, her nails digging into the flesh of her upper arms.

Ryan's head jerked up as he stabbed the photo with his index finger. "This is the same picture you have in your wallet. What the hell are you doing with a picture of one of the Phone Book Killer's victims in your wallet? Who is she?"

She dragged in a shaky breath and closed her eyes. "She's my mother."

Chapter Twelve

Ryan blinked. Her mother. Her mother was that cool blonde on her laptop. She'd told him this woman was her grandmother. He grabbed the picture and held it close to his face.

Grandmother? How could he be so stupid? Judging by the woman's hair and clothing, this photo belonged to the eighties. This woman was too young to be Kacie's grandmother—but not too young to be her mother.

He reread the label in the corner of the picture, the label that tagged this woman as a homicide victim.

The Phone Book Killer had murdered Kacie's mother twenty years before. The reality of it slammed against his chest, knocking the breath from his lungs.

He hunched over the table, flattening his hands against the surface on either side of the picture. The aches and pains of the car accident flooded his body until he became a single ball of hurt.

"Ryan."

He turned his head, and his eyes flicked over the naked woman standing before him, her arms crossed over her perfect body. Her delectable breasts heaving with every harsh breath. Her lush, lying lips parted and moist.

His hands bunched into fists on the table and a muscle in his jaw ticked wildly. He swallowed the rage at how she could keep something like this from him that threatened to overtake all his senses.

He cleared his throat to make sure he could speak. "Why did you want to write this book about my father?"

She brushed a hand across her face and trailed unsteady fingers through the tangles of her hair. "It's a good story, Ryan."

"Don't—" he held up his hand "—lie. And for God's sake, put some clothes on."

She pivoted and scooped up the pajama bottoms he'd removed from her body, inch by seductive inch, a million years before. She stepped into them and dug through the covers to pull out her pajama top. She pulled it over her head and sank to the edge of the bed.

"I wanted to write this book to get to the truth, to exact justice for my mother."

"I said, stop lying." He smacked his open hand against the desk, and the photo of the beautiful dead woman floated to the floor once again. "You thought you already had the truth, and you came here to crucify my father. Why else would you be lying to me all this time about your mother? You came here to put the nail in the coffin of his reputation. You came here to trick me, to use me."

She pinned her hands between her bouncing knees. "You're right. I thought your father was guilty of murdering my mother, but it wasn't my plan to trick you."

"But you did." He smacked his forehead with the heel of his hand, welcoming the pain. "The night before last and last night, too, you came on to me. You did it to get access to my room and this box."

He gave the box a vicious kick, and it flew in the air a foot before landing on its side, spilling its guts.

He laughed and the sound grated against his throat. "You were sloppy. When you filched the photo from the box, you should've run into the hallway and buried it in the trash can by the elevator. Flushed it down the toilet. Ripped it into small pieces and swallowed it. Instead, you put it in your purse."

"I wanted to tell you about my mother, Ryan, because I'd changed my mind. I realized that your father wasn't the Phone Book Killer."

"You wanted to tell me, so you stole the picture from the file and hid it in your purse? Uh-huh."

"I was going to tell you later."

He snorted. "You mean after you got me in bed a few more times and had me so crazy in lo…lust I wouldn't care that you lied to me from the start?"

She covered her face with both hands and her shoulders shook. He ground his back teeth as his natural instinct to comfort her flooded his chest.

Her muffled words came out on a sob. "I wanted to tell you, but I didn't know how. It seemed the damage had already been done."

"You're right. You should've been straight with me from the beginning. You could've come to me with the truth. I would've understood."

She hopped up from the bed. "You never would've agreed to work with me, and I didn't know you, didn't know anything about you. You were the enemy. Do you know how many years the name Brody filled me with rage? I thought your father had killed my mother. Everything I read about the case pointed to him. I wanted to be the one to prove it once and for all and bring some peace to my mother and the other victims of the Phone Book Killer."

She folded her hands behind her back and leaned against the wall, looking small and defenseless in her pajamas and bedhead hair.

She'd lost her mother as a child in the vilest way. The

Phone Book Killer had turned her world upside down and decimated the only family she had. She must've been adopted soon after that and taken away from her home and everything she knew. No wonder she hated the name Brody.

She must've read his softened expression because she stretched her hand out to him. "I'm so sorry, Ryan. I know now I never should've kept my identity a secret from you. And last night, the night before...there was no pretense. I could've found a million different ways to get into that box."

His jaw tensed. She'd crept around his room not once, but twice while he'd lain sleeping, naked, totally at her mercy in every way.

He pinched the bridge of his nose. "I need to be alone right now. This association, this project—it's over."

She sagged against the wall.

He turned his back on her. "If you need some kind of protection, I can call hotel security to check on you."

"I'm sure I'll be fine in the hotel."

She moved stiffly toward the desk and grabbed her purse. She left the photo of her mother on the floor.

When the door closed behind her, Ryan reached for the phone. He punched in the extension for the front desk and requested some security for Kacie's room. He explained how she'd been the guest locked in the sauna earlier in the week. Still fearing some kind of legal action, the manager agreed readily.

He swooped down and snatched up the photo. He fell across the bed on his back, holding the picture of Kacie's mother in front of his face. She smiled at him with Kacie's lips and reproached him with Kacie's eyes.

He tossed the picture onto the floor and rolled onto his stomach, scrunching a pillow into his face.

His hand skimmed a bit of lacy material and he pulled it from under the pillow. Kacie's silky thong tangled around his fingers, tying him up, binding her to him. He pressed it to his face and inhaled her scent.

He might be mad as hell about her deception, but it didn't make him want her any less.

THE TEARS BURNED hot trails down her face, stinging the abrasion on her cheek. On the floor of her hotel room, Kacie leaned her forehead on her knees, which were pulled to her chest, and her tears dripped off the end of her nose.

As soon as she'd gained a measure of Ryan Brody, the man, she should've told him the truth. Even when she still believed Joseph Brody was the Phone Book Killer and her mother's murderer, she should've come clean to Ryan. He might've ended the project then, but anything would've been better than the look on his face when he realized the truth. He actually believed she'd used him sexually to get to the folder in his room. She'd been speaking the truth, for once, when she'd told him that there were a million different ways she could've gotten her hands on her mother's picture.

She didn't need to land him in bed to do that. She'd *wanted* to land him in bed. If he really thought she'd been faking it with him, he must think she deserved an Academy Award.

She rubbed her hand beneath her runny nose and fell to her side. What did it matter now? She'd blown it. She'd blown the book. She'd blown any chance of discovering her mother's real killer. She'd blown a budding relationship with a decent man.

All because she hadn't trusted that man with the truth. Mom, her adoptive mom, had told her she'd regret not learning to open up more. When her parents had first adopted her, they'd sent her to a child therapist. She'd attended almost a year's worth of sessions before she began to feel comfortable with her new family. Then when she'd hit adolescence, her parents had sent her for another round of head shrinking when it became apparent she was playing fast and loose with the truth when she thought the truth would expose her to someone's displeasure.

Her therapist had diagnosed her with abandonment issues, and she'd been able to work through most of those feelings, but she'd never completely resolved them.

Now it had cost her—big-time.

She curled tighter into her fetal position and allowed the tears to flow unabated.

Someone tapped on the door and she rolled to her back, her pulse jumping in her throat. Had Ryan forgiven her? Was he going to give her a second chance?

She sprang to her feet and peered through the peephole. The disappointment at seeing a room-service waiter punched her in the gut.

"I didn't order any room service."

"I know, ma'am. Mr. Ryan Brody in room 582 ordered it for you."

"He did?" Her voice squeaked like a schoolgirl's. He did care. Maybe he was coming up to join her now.

She pulled open the door, smiling through her tears at the uniformed hotel employee in the hallway. A dark shape lunged from the side, and with a sickening thud, the waiter dropped to the ground.

Kacie choked out a scream and took a backward step into the room. Then she felt a prick on the inside of her wrist and she descended into blackness.

RYAN PACED THE FLOOR, tapping his phone against his palm. Why wouldn't Kacie be answering her hotel phone or her cell phone?

When she'd left his room, she'd been shaken up—not even dressed.

Once she was out of his sight, his worries began to build up. When the hospital called to tell him Cynthia Phelps was still in a coma, he couldn't shake off his concerns, no matter how infuriated he was at Kacie. He'd decided to at least check in by phone.

But she wouldn't answer her phone. It would be one thing if she was just ignoring his number on her cell, but he'd called her from his room phone, too, just in case. And it was highly unlikely she'd ignore a call from a number she didn't recognize. Not with her many true-crime contacts out there.

He shoved his key card in his back pocket and headed for the door. He jogged down the steps of the stairwell to the next floor and pushed through the fire door.

Adrenaline crashed through his body when he saw the crumpled body of a waiter in front of Kacie's hotel door.

He ran to the young man's inert form while digging his cell phone from his pocket. The kid had a lump the size of a melon on the side of his head and copious amounts of blood soaked the carpet beneath him.

He shouted into the phone for the front desk to call 911 and be on the lookout for a woman in duress, possibly in the company of a man.

He jumped to his feet and ran back to the stairwell. He wouldn't have taken her down the elevator since it opened right onto the busy lobby. If he had a gun to Kacie's back, he'd be taking a big risk going through the public place.

He knew this stairwell led to a side door and an alley to the street. His legs pumped like pistons as he ran down the stairs, taking about three at a time.

He heard a door slam below him and vaulted over the handrail, landing on the floor below. He started yelling, his shouts echoing in the stairwell. He needed to cause as much commotion as possible. It was still broad daylight.

He kicked through the final door, which led to a short hallway and a glass security door to the street. He yanked that open and stumbled onto the sidewalk, blinking in the sunlight.

The sight in front of him caused his heart to skip a bit. A man with a black stocking cap on his head was staggering down the alley, carrying Kacie's limp form in his arms.

Ryan shouted and sprinted toward him.

The man hit the sidewalk and dropped Kacie. He ran into the street, dodging cars. Ryan reached Kacie, her body unconscious on the sidewalk. He hovered over her as he watched her abductor hop over a fence and dart between two buildings.

He took a step into the street and Kacie moaned.

He couldn't leave her. He dropped to his knees and gathered her to his chest. "Kacie, Kacie."

He could hear the sirens arriving around the corner at the front of the hotel for the room-service waiter. He scooped up Kacie in his arms and carried her back through the side door of the hotel, past the stairwell and into the lobby.

A woman gasped. "Is she okay?"

"Not at all." He yelled for the front-desk clerk, and a few minutes later one of the EMTs who'd arrived earlier returned to the lobby.

"Was she hit on the head, too?" The EMT snapped on his gloves and lifted Kacie's eyelid.

"I don't think so. I didn't see any injuries on her body. Is the kid okay?"

"He'll be fine." He touched the bruise on Kacie's cheek. "What's this?"

"Air bag. We were in a car accident yesterday. She's going to be all right, isn't she?"

"I think she was drugged. I called for another ambulance. We're taking both of them in. Do you know what happened?"

"From the looks of it, someone used the kid to get her to open her door and then snatched her. I caught the culprit on the sidewalk outside, but he dropped her and took off. I would've gone after him, but I couldn't leave her unconscious on the sidewalk."

The man patted his shoulder. "Of course not."

An hour later, Ryan shifted in the plastic chair, stretching his legs in front of him. He jumped to his feet when the SFPD officer entered the room.

"She's okay?"

"She's gonna be fine." Officer Schrader scratched his chin. "What is it with you, Brody? Small-town chief of police comes to the big city, and violence and mayhem follow."

"It's this book, Schrader. It's my father's case. Someone doesn't want it reopened."

"That's what Sean thought, too. I don't know what's going on."

"Was Kacie able to give you a description of the man who abducted her?"

"Nope. But the waiter said the man corralled the waiter from another floor, forced him at gunpoint to go to Ms. Manning's room and stand at her door with his cart. When she saw he was hotel staff, she opened the door. The assailant, who was wearing a ski mask, hit the kid on the side of the head with the butt of his gun and injected Ms. Manning with a sedative. He then carried her down the stairwell."

"Did you check out the cars on that block? I'm sure he didn't intend to carry an unconscious woman in pajamas through the streets of the city. He must've had a car waiting for him."

"We're running them now. Did you get a look at him?"

"He never turned around. He heard me yelling and dropped her. I could see the black cap on his head. He must've still had the ski mask over his face. He seemed to be moving slowly, having difficulty carrying Kacie."

The officer nodded. "Deadweight's a bitch."

"Can I see her?"

"Ask the doc, but I'm done questioning her for now."

He had no intention of checking with anyone. He had let Kacie down. He never should've allowed her to return to her room by herself, hotel security or no hotel security.

He slipped through the automatically opening doors as two orderlies pushed a patient on a gurney through. He threaded his way through the emergency-treatment area, which was crammed with stretchers and harried doctors in white coats dashing from one curtained area to another.

Ryan peeked behind each curtain, backing away from patients in varying degrees of discomfort.

"Hey, you're not supposed to be back here." A nurse waved a pen at him.

Flashing his badge, he said, "I'm looking for Kacie Manning."

She shrugged and squeezed past him.

Behind the very next curtain, he found Kacie, her coppery hair gleaming against the white pillow and framing her white face.

She turned a pair of saucer-round eyes on him.

He grabbed a plastic chair by the side of her bed and straddled it. He took her limp, cold hand in his. "How are you feeling?"

Her tongue darted out of her mouth. "How did you know something was wrong? How did you know he had me?"

"I didn't know until I saw the waiter knocked out in front of your door."

"What made you come?"

"I felt uneasy." He lifted his shoulders. "I'd called hotel security to do a few extra rounds past your room, but the hospital had just called me to report that Cookie was still unconscious, and it reminded me of the danger you still faced."

She curled her fingers around his hand. "Ryan, I'm so sorry I didn't tell you about my mother."

"Let's leave that for now." He squeezed her hand. "The cop told me you didn't get a look at the man who abducted you. Ski mask?"

"Yes." With her free hand, she smoothed out the wrinkles on the sheet covering her stomach. "All I remember is his cold hand as he grabbed my arm and shoved a needle into it."

"You went out immediately?"

"Yeah. I don't remember a thing after that pinprick."

"He carried you down the stairwell and out the side door to the street. He was heading down the alley with you. I'm sure he had a car parked on the street. He couldn't very well have carried you down the sidewalk."

"Are the police checking on that?"

"They are now."

"He got away."

He released her hand and plowed his fingers through his hair. "I had a choice between leaving you unconscious on the sidewalk and going after him. I chose you."

"After what I did to you? If you had caught up with him, he could've given us answers."

"I wasn't going to leave you lying on the sidewalk, unprotected. For all we know, he could've been working with an accomplice, and someone else could've snatched you."

She folded her arms across her chest and hunched her shoulders. "Why did he want to kidnap me? Why didn't he just kill me in the hotel if he wants me to stop writing this book?"

"I don't know, Kacie. Maybe it was a warning. Maybe he was going to try to find out how much you knew first." He scooted his chair closer. "Did you notice anything about his hands or body before he injected you?"

She bit her lower lip. "He was covered from head to toe in black. I didn't see his hands. I just felt them on my skin."

"Was he tall? When I saw him, he was carrying you and running. He seemed to be struggling."

"I didn't notice his height, but the struggling makes sense if he's running with a woman in his arms."

"A young, fit man wouldn't have been having the same issues."

"Are you trying to say he was old and unfit?"

He sighed and slumped back in the chair. "Just grasping. It still doesn't make any sense to me."

A nurse whipped back the curtain and smacked a clipboard against her hand. "Good news, Kacie. You're out of here."

"Are you sure?" Ryan stood up and faced the nurse. "She was drugged and almost abducted."

"She didn't have much of the drug in her system and we were able to flush out most of it. She might be a little groggy and she shouldn't drive for a few hours, but she's good to go."

Ryan rolled his eyes. "I'll take her back to her hotel."

"I don't have any clothes." Kacie plucked at the paper gown covering her body.

"You have what you came in wearing, right?" The nurse pointed to a plastic bag on a cart in the corner. "Your stuff's in there, and we can give you some slippers."

"I was wearing pajamas."

"Hey, your pj's cover more than what most people wear on the street these days. Nobody's going to notice a thing." She plucked up the plastic bag and dropped it on Kacie's bed.

"Do I need to sign any kind of release form?"

"Right here." The nurse tapped the clipboard and then handed it to Kacie. "We already got your insurance info, so you're free to leave."

When she left, Ryan whistled. "This is another reason why I like Crestview. This place is an assembly line. I'll turn around while you get dressed."

"Nothing you haven't already seen, Brody."

And touched and tasted. He liked hearing that feisty tone back in her voice.

"Along with no shoes, I don't even have any underwear."

"I'm sorry. I should've thought to bring you some clothes when I grabbed your purse from your room."

"I'm glad you had the foresight to get my purse. I swear, I don't think these people would've treated me without a copy of my insurance card."

She ripped open the plastic bag and dumped her pajamas onto the bed. She snatched up the bottoms and wriggled into them beneath the sheet. Then she shrugged out of the paper gown and pulled her top over her head.

He averted his gaze from all that creamy white skin, but she'd had it right. Nothing he hadn't seen before. And felt. And tasted. And enjoyed.

Tossing off the sheet, she said, "I guess I'm ready."

He stood next to the bed and offered his arm, which she took. She rose to her feet, leaning heavily against him.

"Can you walk?"

"Sure." She took a few shuffling steps to prove her point.

"Hang on to me, and I'll get you out of here. I parked my rental car right in front, if they haven't towed me." He curled his arm around her waist and tucked her against his side as he maneuvered through the chaos of the emergency room.

His new rental welcomed them from exactly where he'd left it. He helped Kacie into the passenger seat and then dropped onto the driver's seat.

"You need some food."

"I need a shower first. I haven't had a shower since..." She trailed off, her cheeks sporting two red spots.

He got it. She hadn't had a shower since the day before, when they'd made love. Since before he found out her mother was one of the Phone Book Killer's victims.

"Shower first, then."

In less than an hour they were safely ensconced in her room. This time he didn't leave her alone and wouldn't—no matter how many lies she'd told him.

She stacked a pile of clean clothes in her arms and headed for the bathroom. "Make yourself at home. There's no telling how long I'm going to take in the shower."

"Take as much time as you need, and let me know if you feel dizzy or weak. I'm going to order some room service. Any preferences?"

"Food."

Kacie snapped the bathroom door closed and leaned against it. Where would she be right now if Ryan hadn't saved her? Getting tortured? Beaten like Cookie? Dead? What did that man want with her? He could've killed her in the hallway. Why hadn't he?

It couldn't just be another warning. She and Ryan had gotten that warning the night before in the car—stay away from this case or else.

She dragged the dirty pajamas from her body and tossed

them into the corner of the bathroom, then cranked on the water and stepped into the tub, grabbing the shower curtain as she swayed. Maybe she did need Ryan's help, but he'd probably see it as another ploy to seduce him.

Despite her lie, he had to believe everything she felt, that everything she did with him the previous two nights had come from the heart. He had to believe it, even though she'd given him every reason not to.

She turned her face to the warm spray and let it soothe her skin. He must have felt it, too, that connection between them. Maybe in some weird way, their connection had come from both of them having their lives upended by a serial killer.

She washed her hair and massaged some conditioner into it. Then she soaped up a washcloth and circled it on her skin.

"Are you okay in there?" The knock on the door made her drop the washcloth.

"Yes." She bent over at the waist to retrieve the washcloth from the tub and lurched to the side. "Oh!" She made a grab for the shower curtain, popping a few rings from the rod.

The bathroom door flew open, and Ryan emerged through the steam like some avenging god. "Did you fall?"

He flung back the damaged shower curtain and dropped beside the tub.

Kacie glanced at him from her embarrassing position of all fours in the tub, her hair still goopy with conditioner.

"I—I just dropped the washcloth and had a little trouble picking it up."

"You shouldn't be making any quick moves. And on top of it, you're probably still sore from the wreck yesterday." He placed both hands around her waist. "Sit down."

She rolled back to her bottom, folding her legs beneath her.

Taking the washcloth from her hand, he tapped her knee. "Stretch your legs out so you're flat in the tub. I don't want you toppling over again."

She obeyed and uncurled her legs, stretching them in front of her and scooting back in the tub.

He rose to his knees with the washcloth in his hands and finished the job she had started. She closed her eyes as he rubbed the washcloth across her flesh and down her back. He swirled it in circles down to where her backside met the porcelain. Then he swished it to her front, skimming it across her chest and beneath her breasts.

Now she really felt dizzy and it had nothing to do with that drug.

He dabbed her belly and flicked the washcloth between her legs and then swept it down the insides of her thighs.

He finished with her feet, massaging each toe as if she were some great work of art that needed precise cleaning.

"Can you stand up now to rinse off?"

After that sensuous washing, the only thing she wanted to do now was lie down—with him, on a bed, naked.

"Yes. Really, Ryan, you don't have to do this."

"Yeah, I do. Hang on to me."

She grasped his arm and he helped her stand.

He flicked up the lever for the shower and kept one arm firmly around her waist.

"You're going to get all wet."

"Too late. Rinse out your hair and I'll keep hold of you so you don't lose your balance again."

She let the water run across her body to rinse off the soap and then ducked her head in the spray.

Ryan turned off the water for her and with one arm reached for her towel on the rack.

Was he going to dry her off, too?

He tousled her hair first and then rubbed and blotted the towel across the rest of her body.

He could have taken her again, right against the wall. She wouldn't have fainted or fallen or lost her balance, but she might have screamed.

He flipped down the lid of the toilet and helped her from the tub. "Sit here and finish drying off—and leave this door open."

"You're soaking wet."

He glanced down at the T-shirt clinging to his chest and peeled it off in a single motion.

"There. Feel better?"

Moisture glistened on his smooth skin, enhancing the hard planes of muscle that shifted across his chest.

She swallowed. "Much."

"Holler if you need me. Room service should be here any minute." He stepped out of the bathroom, his wet T-shirt flung over one shoulder.

She finished drying herself and wrapped her hair in the damp towel. As she finished dressing, she heard a knock at the door. Ryan wouldn't open it and had the waiter leave the tray outside.

Did he think her abductor would try the same trick twice? After what had been going on, she'd been a fool to open the door to the waiter in the first place. She hadn't been thinking straight. She'd been excited at the thought of Ryan sending room service to her.

Heck, that shower scene had been a hundred times better than room service.

He called out, "Food's here. Are you doing okay?"

She checked her reflection in the mirror and shoved her damp hair from her face. She'd dry it after she ate.

She stepped into the room and spread her arms. "Presentable at last."

He grunted. "I thought you were damned presentable in the tub."

She ignored the comment. If they allowed this sexual tension to build between them again, there was only one outcome—bed. And she couldn't go there with him, not now. Not until they squared things between them.

"Smells good. What did you order?" She lifted the silver lid from a plate.

"Hamburgers, French fries and some salad, because you're always eating salad."

"The point is to eat salad instead of hamburgers and French fries, not in addition to." She snagged a French fry from the plate and bit into its salty, greasy goodness.

"After what you've been through, you deserve hamburgers, French fries *and* salad."

He dug into his own food, and she layered her burger with tomato, onion and pickles and took a big bite.

It tasted like heaven—calories be damned.

"Did you get any ibuprofen in the emergency room?"

"No. Don't they charge about twenty-five dollars for one pill?"

He shook a small bottle. "I have them for free. Aren't you still sore from the accident last night?"

She was sore from a lot of things. "I'll take one with my burger."

Ryan tapped one onto her plate and continued destroying his cheeseburger.

She finished her food and patted her mouth with a napkin. "I feel halfway human now."

"Good." He stacked his plate and hers onto the tray and poured himself another glass of iced tea from the pitcher. "Now tell me about your mother."

Her eye twitched above her bruised cheek, and she rubbed it. Guess he hadn't forgotten about her little lie.

"What do you want to know?"

"Her name, for starters."

"It's all in the file on the victims."

He shoved the tray out of the way. "I want to hear it from you—all of it."

"Her name was Layla French."

"Where's your biological father?"

The knife twisted in her gut. "I don't know. His name was Russ Langford, and he wasn't around. She'd always told me it was just the two of us. I always got the impression she'd never told him about me. Anyway, after my mother's murder, he never stepped up and I never gave him another thought."

"And the Mannings adopted you."

"I had no other family after the Phone Book Killer took my mom away from me." She sniffed but refused to let the tears fall. He'd see them as a ploy for sympathy. "The Mannings lived here, heard about my plight and petitioned to adopt me. Since there was nobody else beating down my door, Child Protective Services allowed the adoption. Then we moved to Seattle."

"Do you remember anything about your mother's murder?"

"She was here one day and gone the next. When my adoptive mom explained to me years later that Layla had been murdered, she told me that she'd been killed trying to help someone."

He nodded. "That's right. The Phone Book Killer used plaster to put his arm in a cast and then pretend he needed help."

"I just always like to picture it that way—she went out thinking she was lending someone a hand."

"And you always believed that someone was Detective Joseph Brody."

"Everything I ever read pointed to his guilt. Why would he jump from the Golden Gate Bridge at the height of the investigation if he wasn't guilty?"

"I've wondered that a million times." He rubbed his jaw and clasped his chin. "But why would someone threaten us for researching and writing this book if he were guilty?"

"That's what got me, Ryan. That's what changed my mind."

"Then why didn't you tell me about your mother?"

They were back to that. "Honestly?"

"Let's try that first—for a change."

She winced. "Because I wanted to protect myself. I knew how bad it would look if you found out."

"You figured I'd put the brakes on this project."

"I figured you'd put the brakes on us."

"And if there ever was going to be an us, exactly when did you figure you could safely tell me you'd believed at one point my father murdered your mother and you were out to prove it?"

She twisted her wet hair around one hand and studied the ends. "Maybe when we were bouncing grandkids on our knees."

His phone began to ring beside the glass and she nodded toward it.

"You'd better get that." It would save her from explaining herself any further. She'd spent two nights with the man and saw grandkids in their future. The embarrassing part of all that was she meant every word.

He looked at the lit display of his phone. "It's my department. Hey, Paul, whaddya got for me?"

His eyes narrowed to green slits and Kacie caught her breath. More bad news? Her aching body couldn't take any more.

"I see. Yeah, nothing we can do about that."

He ended the call and tapped his phone against his chin.

"Well?" She sat on the edge of her chair, gripping the sides.

"They did a trace on that blocked number on Cookie's phone."

"Who is it? Who called Cookie twice before she was attacked?"

"We don't know."

She slumped. "That's not helpful at all."

"We don't know who called because the trace goes back to a protected phone number."

"A protected phone number? What does that mean?"

"It's like classified information. Whoever called Cookie that day is someone in a position of authority. Seems Cookie had friends—or enemies—in high places."

Chapter Thirteen

"That doesn't mean this person in authority is the one who beat her."

"No, but it's another puzzle piece. Why would someone like that be using a protected number to call a Realtor? You'd think anyone house hunting would want to make communication as easy as possible."

"What kinds of people have these numbers?"

"Politicians, diplomats, police officers."

Kacie brushed some crumbs from the table and tipped them onto the tray. "I think we need to get to work on Christina's research."

"Did I say I wanted back on this project?"

"We can't stop now, Ryan. Don't give up on clearing your father's name because I betrayed you. It looks like we both finally have an opportunity to bring justice to our parents. We can't let that go, regardless of what is or isn't between us."

He stood, hoisted up the tray and walked toward the door. Kacie darted ahead of him and opened it for him.

As much as he wished there was nothing between them at this point, he couldn't deny his attraction to her. Hell, the smallest sound from the bathroom had him bursting into her shower. He knew what he'd find in there and he hadn't been able to stop himself. He'd wanted her smooth skin beneath his hands again. He'd wanted to climb into the tub with her and hold her, keep her safe.

He stood in the center of the room, hands on his hips. "Okay, let's go through Christina's research—together this time. I'll run up and get the box and you stay here, behind a locked door. Do not open it for anyone. I don't care if there are twenty room-service waiters outside bearing gifts."

"If I'm not opening the door, you'd better take this." She handed him her key card and he slipped it in his back pocket.

Five minutes later, he returned with the box in his arms and balanced it on his hip as he unlocked Kacie's door. He held his breath as he walked into the room, but she was sitting cross-legged on the bed, looking at her phone.

"Are you feeling up to this?"

She dropped her phone and snapped her fingers. "Bring it on. I'll be shuffling through some papers. It's not like we're doing hard manual labor."

"It's hard psychological labor." He tapped his head.

He joined her on the bed but put the box firmly between them.

"We can work at the desk if you like. I'm not so weak that I can't sit up in a chair."

"You may not be, but I am." He pinched his neck where it met his shoulder. "I'm still plenty sore from the car crash."

She reached behind him and plumped up an extra pillow. "Lean back."

Before he did, he grabbed a stack of files from the box and dropped them in his lap. "Let's start with the first victim."

"That would be my mother."

"I know, and I'm sorry, Kacie." He reached across the box and brushed the back of his hand along her cheek. "I never even told you that. I was so outraged that you'd kept your identity a secret from me, I never expressed my sympathy for your loss."

"We both lost, Ryan." She blinked her wide eyes. "I didn't expect your sympathy under the circumstances."

"Well, you have it. I'll take her case and you can look at the second murder victim, which is about the time the killer started contacting my father. Maybe a little distance and different perspective will do us both good."

He read through the file silently. Kacie's mother had been a waitress in the Lower Haight, at a seedy joint called the Hippy Shake, where the waitresses went topless more often than not. He slid a gaze at Kacie, who was engrossed in her own reading.

Layla French, if that was even her real name, had taken her baby daughter and left an abusive relationship with Russ Langford back home in Ohio. The cops contacted the ex-boyfriend, Kacie's father, in Ohio. Once the second murder occurred, the police had dropped the abusive-boyfriend angle.

This first case had seemed like a routine homicide investigation, with his father and his partner, Brett Stillwell, zeroing in on the fine clientele of the Hippy Shake. What had happened to the two Joes?

"Kacie, who was my father's partner on the second case?"

She lifted up the corner of a piece of paper. "Detective Stillwell. Why?"

He scratched his chin with the edge of the paper he was holding. "I always thought my father's partner was named Joe, like him. They called my father Joey and his partner Joe to avoid confusion."

"Could be Joe Stillwell. His first name isn't listed, or I haven't gotten to that part yet."

"I have. It's Brett Stillwell." He slid his phone from the nightstand and punched in Sean's number. His brother answered after two rings.

"What's up, Ry?"

Sean had given his department strict orders not to disturb him, so he knew nothing about the trouble—including the fact that Kacie Manning was the daughter of a murder victim—and Ryan intended to keep it that way.

He cleared his throat. "We're going through Christina's files and I have a question for you."

"Shoot."

"Who was Dad's partner in homicide?"

"For most of his career or during the Phone Book Killer investigation?"

"For most of his career."

"Joe Rigoletto. Joey and Joe."

"Why didn't he work this case with Dad? He was working with a Brett Stillwell instead."

"Joe Rigoletto was dead by the time of the first Phone Book murder."

"Dead?"

Kacie was peering at him over the top of the box, and he tapped Speaker for her.

Sean continued. "He died on the job, beside Dad. They were investigating a couple of murders related to a suspected drug dealer. They got a tip on the guy's whereabouts, and they were ambushed. Dad escaped injury but Joe wasn't so lucky. Happened about six months before the first Phone Book murder."

Kacie sucked in a breath.

"Who was that?"

"That was Kacie Manning." He glanced at the papers spread out on the bed. "We're working."

Sean shouted across the line. "Hey, Kacie, we're all looking forward to meeting you someday."

"Likewise."

"Is that it, Ry? Because I've got a lady waiting for me poolside."

"Yeah, and I can't wait to meet the woman who loosened Sean Brody up enough to get him to take an extended vacation."

"You'll meet Elise soon enough. You're gonna love her. She's sweet, straightforward, uncomplicated, honest—not at all like… Well, you'll meet her."

"Looking forward to it."

They ended the call and Ryan cupped the phone between his hands, his brow furrowing.

"She sounds like a paragon of virtue," Kacie offered.

"Huh? Who?"

"Elise." Kacie flipped back her hair along with another page of the file. "Sounds like a regular Mother Teresa."

"Umm, yeah. I heard from Eric that she's really nice, a kindergarten teacher from Montana or someplace like that. Not Sean's usual type, but then, his usual type never worked out for him."

"And who is this sweet, uncomplicated, *honest* woman not at all like?"

Ryan finally dragged his gaze away from the page in front of him and met Kacie's eyes. "What are you talking about?"

"Your brother, he mentioned on the phone that Elise was not at all like someone. Who's that someone?"

"Our mother. I told you, after Dad's death, she turned to booze and pills and never looked back. Her days were filled with hiding the stuff from us and obtaining it with phony prescriptions. Lies upon lies upon lies."

She looked down at her fidgeting fingers. "So, I guess

it's really important for you Brody boys to be with an honest woman, someone who will never lie to you like your mother did."

He snorted. "You'd think so, wouldn't you? But there's my brother Eric, who took back his fiancée after she kept his daughter from him. Can you imagine?"

"She had a baby with your brother and didn't tell him about it? And he took her back?"

"Extenuating circumstances. She had her reasons, and those two are made for each other—true love and all that."

"Must be nice."

Ryan tapped the tip of his pencil against the side of the box. "Don't you think that's weird?"

"That Eric took her back?"

"What? No. Don't you think it's weird that my dad's longtime partner in homicide died in an incident on the job six months before the case that would bring my dad down?"

"I guess Joey and Joe turned out to be the bad-luck duo."

"You could say that. But why is it that every time I look at this case, I find out something new and disturbing? You know my brother Eric was kidnapped during this case, right?"

"Yes."

"He just found out recently that some coven of witches was involved in his kidnapping."

Kacie hugged a file to her chest. "Do you think they also had something to do with the Phone Book Killer? Maybe he was a member of the coven? I don't remember the occult being associated with any of the slayings."

"It wasn't. I don't know where that leaves us, but I'd like to find out more about Joe Rigoletto's death."

"Marie Giardano?"

"Most likely."

Kacie uncurled her legs and stretched them in front of her, pointing her toes. "By the way, the killer started contacting your dad by leaving packages at the station for him. They contained notes with letters cut and pasted from magazines and bits of info about the crimes that only the killer could've known."

His gaze skimmed her calf where her pant leg had risen and settled on her delicate feet with her blue-painted toenails. What were they just discussing?

Notes.

He lined up his spine along the headboard, bumping his head against the wall. "The people who suspected him of being the Phone Book Killer always claimed he'd left those notes himself, maybe to garner publicity."

"Part of what led to their suspicions about him is that nobody ever saw anyone leave those notes." She crossed her legs at the ankle and began tapping her toes together.

Was she trying to torture him?

"Then they found some plaster in his car, suggesting he might have been making his own arm brace, just like the Phone Book Killer did." Ryan crossed his arms behind him, cradling his head against his laced fingers. "There had been one or two witnesses who reported that a man in a cast had been in the area where the victims were abducted."

"But nobody ever ID'd Joseph Brody. I'm not sure there was much of a case against him, just suspicion and innuendo."

He swung his legs off the bed and hunched forward on his knees. "A lot of that came from his own department, the brass."

"Usually a P.D. circles the wagons for one of its own. I thought your dad was a good cop, an excellent detective."

"Maybe they were worried about the stain on the department. From what I remember when Sean used to talk about this stuff all the time, there had been some bribery or something uncovered at the department not too long before these murders. They didn't want to go down that road again, so they jumped on the pithy evidence tying my father to the murders."

Kacie spread her hands. "There's so much here, I can't believe I ever thought your father was the Phone Book Killer."

"There's still a lot that doesn't add up. The biggest mystery of all is why he killed himself if he wasn't guilty."

"Maybe it had nothing to do with the case. Did you ever consider that possibility? Maybe he was ill or in some kind of other trouble. Gambling debts? Some kind of graft? You just said there'd been some trouble with the department prior to the murders."

"I suppose gambling and graft are better than murder."

She shoved a sheaf of papers from her lap and hopped from the bed. "I'm not trying to imply that your father was a criminal. Just looking at other possibilities. I spent too long with tunnel vision, believing what I wanted to believe."

"No offense taken. Just be honest with me, Kacie. That's all I ask."

"I swear, no more secrets." She drew a cross over her heart. "Back to the station tomorrow to conduct a follow-up? I want to know if they have any leads on Duke Bannister's murder."

"Then there's the attack on Cookie."

"There are so many loose ends, it's making me dizzy."

Closing her eyes, she massaged her temples and Ryan was at her side in a nanosecond. "Sit down. Let me get you some water."

She opened one eye and skewered him with it. "It was a figure of speech. I'm not really dizzy."

He squeezed her shoulders and laughed…and it felt good.

She felt good. "That's what you said when you headed into the bathroom, and look what happened in there."

"I toppled over reaching for the washcloth. It could've happened to anyone. I didn't need a shower assistant."

"I didn't hear you complaining." He raised one eyebrow at her, his blood stirring again.

"Who in their right mind would complain about…that?"

He traced her jaw with his thumb and then dropped his hands and stepped back. Could he trust this woman? Eric may have forgiven Christina for a much more egregious lie, but those two had history. He'd just met Kacie a week before, and she'd been lying to him from the get-go. What other secrets did she have up her sleeves?

She crossed her arms, tucking her fists against her body. "So, we'll meet tomorrow morning and head to the station?"

"You're not getting rid of me. I made a mistake leaving you on your own this morning."

Golden sparks flew from her eyes and her lush lips parted as her breath quickened.

"I'll bunk on the floor."

Her mouth snapped closed, and she compressed her lips into a thin smile. "Afraid I'll seduce you with my wicked, wicked ways?"

"Nope." He reached past her, grabbed two pillows and threw them on the floor. "I'm afraid of what I'll do to you."

WHAT HAD HE meant by being afraid of what he'd do to her? Kacie rolled onto her left side again to peer at the large, slumbering form on her hotel-room floor.

What did she know about Chief Ryan Brody anyway? One week before, she'd believed he was the third son of a serial killer, a killer who'd murdered her mother.

And now? Now she couldn't imagine her life without

him. She punched her pillow before scrunching it beneath her head. She'd come into this thing planning to remain cool, calm and collected. She'd pump Brody for information and tell her story, her way.

She'd been able to do that with a sociopath like Daniel Walker, but all her reason had flown out the window the minute Ryan had gathered her in his strong arms.

With thoughts of the murders spinning in her head and her sexy protector on the floor next to her, sleep was long in coming.

The next morning, Kacie woke up to the sound of the shower. She bolted upright. Ryan had packed up his makeshift bed, stacking the two pillows on the chair and folding the blanket on top of them.

Maybe if she heard a bump in the shower, she could come to his rescue. She'd be the best damned shower assistant he ever had. She'd soap up every inch of his body, not once but twice. She'd even climb in there with him. She'd kneel before him with the warm spray pounding her back, and she'd...

"Earth to Kacie."

She glanced up to find the object of her desire leaning out of the bathroom door, fully clothed. "I'll be done in a few minutes. Are you feeling okay?"

"I'm fine." Considering he'd just ruined a perfectly good daydream.

"Still sore?"

"Nothing a little pain reliever can't cure." And a warm shower with a special helper.

"I'll leave the bottle by the sink in here. I had to pop a few more myself. I think those air bags can do more damage than a steering wheel to the chest." He raised his inner forearms, which were still bruised by the air bag.

"Ouch."

"Do you mind if we stop off at my room so I can change into some clean clothes?"

"No problem." She stepped past him into the bathroom and started to swing the door closed.

He stopped it with his hand. "Are you steady on your feet now?"

Should she tell him another lie and say that she was about ready to collapse?

"I've had a good night's sleep and I'm fine. I'll leave the door unlocked if it makes you feel better."

"It would."

He removed his hand and she closed the door with a snap. She'd actually just told him another lie anyway. She did *not* have a good night's sleep.

She stepped into the tub and turned her back to the water. How could she have possibly slept with Ryan sprawled on her floor?

They could've shared the bed and kept their hands to themselves. She soaped up her hands and rubbed her body, her eyelashes fluttering. Who was she kidding? She wouldn't have been able to keep her hands to herself. Maybe if they laid a brick wall down the middle of the bed.

Ryan tapped on the door. "Doing okay in there?"

"Yeah, yeah."

"Is that what you call a short shower?"

It would've been short if she hadn't started daydreaming again and pretending her hands were Ryan's. They were a poor substitute anyway.

She turned off the water and toweled off before climbing out of the tub. She dressed in the bathroom and wiped the steam from the mirror with the towel, then pushed open the bathroom door and called into the other room. "We need to make a list of what to ask at the station. We've got the doll, Bannister's murder, Cookie's attack…"

He finished for her. "My car, your abduction and some questions for Marie about Joe Rigoletto."

She poked her head out of the bathroom. "Do you think the cops will run us out of town on a rail after all that?"

"I just know this all would've been easier if my brother were here."

"He'd come back if you called him, wouldn't he?"

"Sure, he would, but it's been so long since the guy's had a real vacation and even longer since he's had a real woman. My brothers and I have been telling him for years to relax, and now that he's finally taken our advice, I'm not going to reel him back in."

"Then you're doing the right thing. And he does have allies in the department."

"John Curtis. We can count on him."

"Then let's get going, after stops for clean clothes and breakfast."

When they hit the station, they made the rounds. The lab had gotten nothing from the doll that Daniel Walker denied ever sending to her, and the detectives had no leads on Bannister's murder or the attack on Cookie Phelps, who was still in a coma.

"Give me something, John." Ryan crossed his arms as he perched on the end of Detective Curtis's desk. "What about my car?"

"Aha!" Curtis held up one finger as he shuffled through some papers on his messy desk. "Your brake lines were cut."

"I figured that. Any idea who did it?"

"Someone who followed you to that taco stand in South San Francisco."

"That's brilliant. No wonder my brother insists on working with you."

"Ouch," John said with mock pain. "You small-town cops have no idea the pressures we face in the big city."

"I'll give you one more chance. Anything on the guy who tried to abduct Kacie?"

Curtis shook his finger at Ryan and smiled at Kacie. "You see? I was saving the best for last."

Kacie's pulse jumped. "You found him?"

"Not quite. Follow me to Lieutenant Healy's office. We got something from the hotel video camera."

Kacie squealed and grabbed Ryan's arm. "Finally."

"Don't get your hopes up. It's pretty grainy, but maybe you'll recognize the guy."

They approached Lieutenant Healy's office and Curtis knocked. "Brody and Ms. Manning are here to look at the video."

Healy looked up from his desk. "What the hell is going on here, Brody?"

"I guess someone doesn't want Ms. Manning to write this book."

"Drugging and kidnapping her is an odd way to stop her." He steepled his fingers and peered at Kacie over the pinnacle. "Are you sure this isn't related to your other book, Ms. Manning? The panic over the doll. Bannister's warning from Daniel Walker. Isn't this just more of the same?"

"I don't think so. Walker doesn't know or have any interest in Cynthia Phelps."

"Ah, but Cookie's predicament could be due to her past as a hooker. Some pimps never forget."

"If we can get to the bottom of all these attacks, maybe that's exactly what we'll discover, but we need to get to the bottom of them first."

He spun his laptop around to face them. "Then start here. Do you recognize that man? We're pretty sure he's the one who forced the hotel employee to deliver that room service to your door and then jabbed you with a needle."

She bent forward at the waist and squinted at the grainy footage. A middle-aged man with graying hair and what looked like a scarf around his neck loped through a side door of the hotel.

"Is that the best you got?"

"That's it, but if you look at his neck, that could be his ski mask pulled down."

"Yes, I see that."

"The hotel is sure he's no guest, and the timing of his entrance into the hotel matched the timing of your abduction."

"Wait—play it again and stop it when he turns his face to the side."

She stared at the profile of the man who'd drugged her and forcibly removed her from the hotel and felt—nothing. He was a stranger. Grayish hair curled at the nape of his neck, and his prominent nose might make him stand out from a crowd, but she didn't recognize him.

She turned to Ryan. "Have you ever seen him before?"

"Nope."

"Oh well, at least it's something. I'd probably recognize him if I saw him again, so he's lost the element of surprise."

Healy held up a pencil and tested its point. "Why do you suppose he tried to kidnap you?"

"I have no clue, but your tone of voice indicates you might."

Ryan had stepped closer to her, brushing her arm with his. "Let's hear it, Lieutenant."

"Just seems convenient that Brody here was able to rescue you in time, and the perp just drops you and is able to get away, even though he looks about half Brody's size and strength."

Ryan tensed beside her. "Go on."

"Would be a nice little companion story to the release of the book—author gets abducted while writing the true-crime story of the Phone Book Killer."

Ryan clenched a fist, and she covered it with her hand. "Yeah, okay, I want another bestseller so badly I'm willing to hire someone to bash a poor kid on the side of the head and inject me with a horse tranquilizer. Save your theories for the movie script, Lieutenant, and just do your job."

Curtis glared while Healy snatched his laptop. "We'll let you know if we discover anything else."

"I'm sure you will." Ryan applied pressure to the small of her back and she turned and walked out of the office.

After they had shut the lieutenant's office door and had walked halfway down the hallway, Kacie sputtered, "What a jackass."

Curtis patted her arm. "That's the lieutenant for you. Don't take it personally."

"Keep us posted, John. You know where to find me."

"You keep us posted, Brody. This whole thing is getting crazy."

Ryan jabbed the button for the elevator. "At least we know what the guy looks like—sort of. I think that hotel needs to upgrade its security cameras."

"They need to upgrade their entire security system. At the rate I'm going there, they'll have to comp me a full year's stay."

He held a finger to his lips. "Shh. Don't give Healy any ideas. He'll probably accuse you of trying to score freebies all over the city next."

"Wouldn't put it past him."

The elevator doors opened on the smiling face of Ray Lopez. He held up his hand in greeting. "How's the book coming along, Kacie?"

"Just fine, thanks."

"Call me if you want a coauthor."

When they got in the elevator, Ryan mumbled, "Talk about jackasses."

When they reached their floor, they opened the door to the records area.

A young blonde with a bright smile greeted them. "Hello. What can I do for you?"

Ryan's eyebrows met over his nose. "Where's Marie?"

"Oh, you haven't heard?" The woman looked both ways as if the boxes surrounding her had ears. "Marie's gone."

Chapter Fourteen

Blood thrumming against his eardrums, Ryan clawed at the mesh screen dividing him from this woman who wasn't Marie.

"What are you talking about? Where is she?"

The woman took a step back. "We don't know. Who are you again?"

Ryan fumbled in his pocket and whipped out his badge and ID. "I'm Ryan Brody, chief of police in Crestview. Detective Sean Brody's my brother."

"Okay, I know you. Anyway, Marie took off. Nobody knows where she went."

"What does that mean?"

"Wait a minute." Kacie tapped her fingertips against his forearm. "You mean she went on vacation?"

Ryan blinked. Maybe it was as simple as that. Just because Marie had been paranoid didn't mean she'd disappeared.

He took a deep breath. "Is that it? She took some time off?"

"I guess so, but she didn't put it on the calendar and she didn't tell anyone."

"What do you mean?" Ryan rattled the cage. "Why are you talking in riddles?"

The woman's skin flushed red. "I don't mean to, sir, but you're not letting me get a word in edgewise."

"She's right." Kacie squeezed his arm. "Let her start from the beginning. What's your name?"

The woman flicked her eyes toward Kacie and licked her lips. "My name's Sheila Moriarty. I'm filling in for Marie. Yesterday she just didn't show up for work."

Ryan opened his mouth, but Kacie pinched his side and he shut it.

"She's usually prompt, so when she still wasn't here by nine o'clock, someone called her at home and on her cell. She didn't answer. One of the officers dropped by her place and it looked like she'd taken off in a hurry. Her closet doors and dresser drawers were standing open. No purse, no phone, no car."

"No signs of violence?" Ryan finally uncurled his fingers from the mesh, but his heart was still pounding against his rib cage.

"Officer Reynolds didn't see any signs of violence. It looks like she left in a hurry."

"Did any neighbors see her leave?"

"You know what?" She grabbed a card and scribbled on it. "I'm going to give you Officer Reynolds's info, and you can ask him all the questions you want. In the meantime, did you come down here for something specific, Chief Brody?"

"Yeah, I came down here to talk to Marie, but since that's not possible, I want to look at anything you have about the on-the-job shooting of a Detective Joe Rigoletto."

Sheila wrinkled her nose as she typed on her keyboard. "That doesn't sound familiar to me. When did that happen?"

"About twenty years ago."

Sheila stopped typing and dropped her jaw. "I don't think I'm going to find that."

"It hasn't been filed electronically yet, but you probably still have the paper files."

"I have no idea how I'd find that." She spread her hands.

"I know Marie's system. Do you want to let us in and we'll give it a shot ourselves?"

She glanced over her shoulder. "I don't know."

"Look, nobody has to know, and I won't even sign your log."

Sheila chewed her bottom lip and then hit the buzzer that unlocked the cage. "I guess so. Just don't tell anyone I let you back here to roam around."

"Believe me, we're not telling anyone."

He placed a hand on Kacie's back and propelled her through the door, just in case Sheila changed her mind.

When they reached the dusty boxes in the back of the room, Kacie whispered, "What do you think happened to Marie?"

"I hope her paranoia got the best of her and she took off for parts unknown for a while. I just wish she would've gone through proper channels. She would've attracted less attention that way."

"Maybe something spooked her."

"There's a lot of that going around." He knocked on one of the boxes on the shelf. "Let's see what we can find."

They took down the files for the year they were looking for and began reading the labels aloud to each other. Then they started spilling into the next year.

Kacie stood on her tiptoes to peer at a box on the top shelf. "Maybe they don't keep the officer-involved shootings or deaths down here."

"Maybe."

"Why don't you ask John? He seems like someone you can trust."

He tugged on his earlobe and narrowed his eyes. "We're

in a police station. Are you implying we can't trust anyone here?"

"Marie didn't."

He ran his eye across the shelf where the file on Rigoletto's shooting should've been. Had someone beat them to it? And if so, why?

Why did nothing seem to add up anymore?

"Another dead end. Seems like we're running into a lot of those."

Kacie took his hand. "Maybe someone up there is trying to tell us something—maybe it's our parents trying to tell us something."

"Are you saying you want to give up on the story?"

She glanced down at their entwined hands. "When I wrote that book on Walker and began to realize he had killed his family, I was scared of facing such evil day after day when I interviewed him. I was afraid of tricking him, and I was afraid of what he'd do when he discovered I'd tricked him. But Walker was a known threat, and he was locked up. I don't know what, or who, I'm facing here."

He pointed to the ceiling. "You have a picture of the man who tried to abduct you."

"And it means nothing. I really don't know if I'd even recognize that face in a crowd. There are other forces at work here." She waved her arm around the records room. "Forces we can't see."

He pulled her close. "I'll be here to protect you, Kacie. You know that, right?"

"I knew it once, before you discovered my true colors."

Did she blame him for her kidnapping? He tightened his hold on her. "I should've never sent you back to your room alone that morning."

Her spine stiffened, and she drew back from his embrace. "That wasn't your fault, Ryan. You know how I got in trouble that morning? I put myself there with my lies. I'm surprised you even came back to check on me. I didn't deserve it. I came into this project with the intent of turning the tables on the sons of Joseph Brody."

"But it didn't work out that way. You were open enough to see the truth."

"It didn't work out that way because I wasn't counting on falling for one of the sons of Joseph Brody."

Did she think she had to tell him that so he wouldn't believe the two nights they'd spent together were a sham?

He brushed the hair from the nape of her neck. "It was all too fast between us."

"And because of that you think it wasn't real?"

He knew it was real on his end, but he wasn't going to open himself up to getting used. "One thing at a time, Kacie. We mixed adrenaline and lust into a high-octane cocktail that exploded in our faces."

Sheila called from the front. "Are you two done back there? I'm ready to lock up for lunch."

Ryan shrugged and said, close to Kacie's ear, "I guess we're done."

She pivoted out of his arms and strode toward the front of the cage. She smiled brightly at Sheila. "That's it for us."

"Didn't find anything?" Sheila's head swiveled from left to right, looking at their empty hands.

"We saw the area where the case files should've been, but they weren't there."

"Well, that's some old stuff." She jingled her keys in her palm as if to remind them she wanted them out.

"Thanks anyway, Sheila—and sorry for coming on so strong before. Marie Giardano's a friend of mine, and I'm a little worried about her sudden departure."

"I understand. We're all a little worried, but it looks like she left of her own free will."

As they walked out of the room, Ryan leaned toward Kacie. "I'm not so sure about that."

When the elevator doors closed, Kacie asked, "Are you going to talk to John Curtis about any of this? Rigoletto? Marie?"

"I was just thinking we should invite John to lunch."

"Sounds like a good idea."

They located John in the squad room and extended their invitation.

"Let me wrap up a few things," he said, "and I'll meet you at the sandwich place down the street. As for Marie, I think she's okay."

Later at the sandwich shop, they found a table. They picked up lunch and a couple of fountain drinks while they waited for John.

Ryan stretched his legs in front of him. "Is your book a complete shambles now?"

"It's not moving in a linear progression, if that's what you mean."

"Did the other one?"

"It was different." She chewed on her straw. "The case had already been solved. Walker had been tried and convicted by the time I wrote the book."

"But didn't you start that book believing he was innocent?"

"I was certainly willing to give him a chance. His defense seemed so compelling."

"How soon after you met him did you begin to doubt him?"

"It wasn't meeting him so much, because he's charming and convincing. It was reviewing the evidence. While the media were busy buying into Walker's B.S., they neglected to reveal some of the true facts of the case. I looked at those facts, and it became pretty clear to me. Then the book became more of a psychological study of Walker."

"The so-called facts of this case are a lot less compelling, aren't they?"

"That's just it—there are very few facts. Plaster in your father's car to make an arm cast? So what? He maintained it was planted, didn't he?"

"Yep."

"And there was no proof it wasn't—no receipts indicating your father purchased the materials, no witnesses putting your father near these victims. Nothing was there really, except the fact that the killer was communicating with your father and then the kicker, that your father jumped from the bridge."

"Yep, that was the kicker."

"Can anyone join this party?" Curtis hovered over the table, balancing a tray with a sandwich and a bag of chips on it.

Ryan kicked out the chair across from him. "Have a seat, John. We were just talking about my father's case."

"What else?" He sat down, unloaded his food from the tray and then twisted around to put the tray on another table.

"First off, what do you know about Marie's disappearance?"

"Not much, but she was dropping some pretty broad hints the day before she left. I think she was trying to tell me not to worry."

"Is this going to hurt her retirement?" Ryan shook the ice in his cup.

"Not if I can help it."

"Do you think she left because of us? Because of this book?"

"I wouldn't say you in particular, but it's been building.

Started with Sean's case. You know, our own fingerprint guy was the Alphabet Killer."

"Yeah, I knew that."

"Then your other brother Eric was out here looking into another set of murders. Nothing to do with your father's case, but he was snooping around in Records, too."

"Speaking of snooping around in Records, Kacie and I just went down there to look up the files on Dad's partner."

"Stillwell?"

"No, the one before that. Rigoletto."

"Killed in the line of duty."

"That's the one."

"Why are you looking into that, Brody?"

"That incident occurred about six months before everything started going downhill for my father."

"And you think they're related?"

"You can't deny it's a coincidence. Two partners dead within six months of each other."

"It happens, Brody. Maybe not in the small town of Crestview, but in the big city it's not uncommon. Lotta stress here."

"That's bull. Stress maybe, but death? Even for a big department like San Francisco's, deaths on the job aren't that common. I know that was before your time, but did you ever hear anything about it?"

"Detective Joseph Rigoletto's picture is hanging on the wall at the station, but I don't know much more about it. I think his widow's still alive and living in the city. Marie knew her."

"Who didn't Marie know?" Kacie balled up the paper from her sandwich and tossed it onto her tray.

"That's the point." Curtis made a gun with his fingers. "She knows too much and maybe that's why she took off."

"Will you help me look her up?"

"Do you mean, will I use the department's resources to locate her for you? Sure. You're my partner's brother. When's he coming back to work, anyway?"

"When he's good and ready."

Back at the station, it didn't take Curtis long to locate Joe Rigoletto's widow. He jotted down her address on a pink message slip and slid it across the desk to Ryan. "You didn't get this from me."

They drove south out of the city to Mrs. Rigoletto's home in the suburbs.

When they pulled to the curb across the street from the neat house, Kacie put a hand on his arm. "Do you think we should burst in on her unannounced? She's elderly, isn't she? Wasn't Rigoletto older than your father?"

"Yeah, but I don't want to give Mrs. Rigoletto a chance to suddenly head out of town on a much-needed vacation."

"Okay, I'll follow your lead."

Ryan knocked on the door. He could tell they were being looked over from the vantage point of the peephole.

He flipped out his badge and held it up. "Mrs. Rigoletto? I'm Chief Ryan Brody. I'd just like to ask you a few questions."

The dead bolt clicked and he blew out a breath.

When the door swung open, he raised his eyebrows. Either Mrs. Rigoletto had aged incredibly well, or Rigoletto had married a much younger woman.

"Mrs. Rigoletto?"

The woman narrowed her eyes. "No, I'm her daughter, Rebecca Leeds."

"I'm Ryan Brody. This is Kacie Manning. We'd like to ask your mother a few questions about your father's incident."

"Brody…?" Rebecca grasped the doorjamb. "I know

who you are. Do you really think delving into my father's death is going to help your father?"

"I don't know. Didn't you ever wonder how it came about that the two partners were both dead within six months of each other?"

"I was in my late twenties when it happened. Dad's death destroyed Mom, and then when your father committed suicide, she fell apart even more."

"Happened to a lot of people."

"I'd met your dad once or twice. He was a great guy. My father always sang his praises. Said he could retire with ease, knowing detectives like Joey Brody were taking his place."

"Does your mother remember much about your father's murder? I tried to find the case file, but I couldn't locate it."

"Does she remember much about my father's murder?" Rebecca widened the door and ushered them into the house. "Follow me."

They trailed after her into an airy, open kitchen where a woman with bright red hair sat at a table with a pair of scissors and magazines spread before her.

"Ma, this is Ryan Brody, Joey Brody's son. Do you remember Joey Brody?"

Mrs. Rigoletto turned a pair of faded blue eyes on him and arched one eyebrow. "Is he the plumber? Because that faucet is still leaking. Or is it a bunker?"

"Is what a bunker?" Rebecca shrugged at Ryan.

"The thing that's leaking."

"It's called a faucet, Ma. You were right the first time. Faucet."

"Are you the plumber?"

Rebecca rubbed her mother's back. "No, I'm Rebecca, your daughter."

"Tell the plumber to fix the bunker."

Rebecca turned the page of one of the magazines. "These are pretty dresses. Cut these out, Ma."

The scissors began to slice through the glossy pages, and Ryan shook his head at Kacie, whose wide eyes glimmered with tears.

Rebecca stepped away from her mother and pulled out a couple of stools at the kitchen island. "My mom can't remember what a faucet is. She's not going to remember what happened twenty years ago."

"I'm sorry, Rebecca."

"Yeah, life's a bitch and then you get Alzheimer's or… worse. Why are you looking into this now?"

Ryan straddled a stool. "Kacie's writing a book about my father. When I discovered his partner, your father, had been killed in a shoot-out six months before everything came down on my dad, I figured we needed to look into it more."

"You're brave, digging into all that old stuff. I like to pack it up and put it away." She glanced at her mother. "In some ways, the memory loss is a blessing."

Kacie asked, "What do you remember about that time, Rebecca?"

"It was an ambush. They were anxious to interview a drug dealer about a couple of murders on his turf. A snitch dimed him off, and your father and mine went out to an abandoned warehouse in the Tenderloin to track him down. They didn't even make it to the door. My father was gunned down in the street and yours took cover behind their car and returned fire, calling it in."

"Did the police ever make an arrest in the case?"

"Oh yeah." She folded her hands on the counter. "Turns out it was the snitch."

Kacie tilted her head. "Why'd he do it?"

"I don't know. Making points on the street? Maybe someone blew his cover and he had to prove himself. He didn't share his motives with us." Rebecca's knuckles turned white. "I only saw him once. He pled out and we went to the courthouse for his sentencing. He had dead eyes. No emotion whatsoever."

Ryan clasped the back of his neck. It was a rare snitch who turned on his benefactors. "Is he still in the joint?"

"He died in there several years ago—shanked. What goes around comes around."

Another death in a long line of them. Another dead end.

Tapping the counter, Ryan said, "Sorry to bother you, Rebecca. Thanks for the info."

She came around the counter and swept scraps of paper from the kitchen table into her hand. "Maybe you should just let it go, Ryan. Nobody who knew Joey Brody believed for one minute he was the Phone Book Killer."

"He did jump off the Golden Gate Bridge."

"That he did."

Mrs. Rigoletto dropped her scissors. "Joey Brody didn't jump off the bridge."

Rebecca crouched beside her mother. "Do you remember Joey Brody, Ma?"

"Is he the plumber?" Her restless, blue-veined hands hovered above her paper-doll cutouts.

Rebecca heaved a sigh, plucked up the scissors and shrugged at Ryan. "I'll call the plumber."

Ryan knelt before Mrs. Rigoletto, who was happily brandishing her scissors again, and placed a hand on her knee. "You take care, Mrs. Rigoletto."

Her face crumpled for a moment, and the blue eyes seemed to focus on his face. "Joey Brody never jumped from that bridge."

Ryan squeezed her knee. "Goodbye."

When they got to the front door, Rebecca waved a hand in the direction of her mother. "Sorry about all that."

"Is she ever lucid?" Kacie stepped onto the porch ahead of him.

"Occasionally. She goes in and out. More out these days."

Kacie took her hand. "Well, bless you for taking care of her."

"Oh, I'm no saint." Rebecca laughed. "There's a passel of Rigolettos, and we all take turns. We have a caregiver, too."

"Then you're all saints. Thanks for your time."

Ryan waved and turned toward the street. "That's gotta be tough. At least my mom recognized us even when she was in a drug-induced haze."

When they got to the car, Kacie pulled out a pad of paper and started jotting down notes.

"Are you putting down what she told us?"

"Every little bit helps. Detective Joe Rigoletto will have a place in this story, even if it doesn't lead us to the truth."

"It doesn't seem as if anything is leading us to the truth."

They drove back into the city, and as always, Ryan caught glimpses of the Golden Gate Bridge as he maneuvered the car through the city streets, cresting the hills. If those barriers on the bridge could talk...

He parked his rental car in the lot below the hotel, and they took the elevator up to the lobby.

As they ambled across the carpet, the hotel clerk, Michael, called to Kacie. "Ms. Manning?"

She pivoted on the carpet and mumbled to Ryan, "Are they going to compensate me for my near-abduction by giving me the hotel?"

"They should."

When they reached the counter, Ryan asked, "How's your employee? The one who got cracked over the head?"

"He's doing fine, but he's spooked."

"I heard he couldn't identify his assailant."

"The guy was wearing a ski mask when he approached him, but he looked at the video and ID'd the guy from his clothing. Hopefully, they can get him from that."

"I'm glad he's okay." Kacie tapped the counter. "Is that why you called me over?"

"No. Actually, someone left you a note at the front desk."

Ryan's pulse picked up. "Who? Did you see him?"

"I wasn't working at the time. We left a message on the phone in your room, but I saw your name on the note and when I noticed you come in I thought I'd save you a trip up to your room and back down here."

"I appreciate it. Do you have the note?"

He stepped back from the counter. "I have the envelope right here." He slapped the white envelope on the counter.

"Thanks." Kacie swept the envelope from the polished wood. She carried it to the collection of love seats where they'd opened the package containing the doll not more than a week before.

She sank to the edge of one of the seats and ripped the envelope open with one finger. She shook out the single piece of paper and gasped.

"What is it?" His fingers itched to snatch it from her hand.

"This may be the lead we're looking for."

"Kacie, what is it?"

She waved the paper at him. "Someone's finally willing to talk, someone who may know the truth."

He couldn't take it anymore. He plucked the note from her fingertips and the words danced before his eyes. *I know the truth and I'm ready to tell all.*

Ryan crumpled the paper in his fist and slammed it against his knee—not at all the reaction she was expecting from him.

"Did you read the rest of it? He wants to meet with me. He left a number."

"Who is this, another Duke Bannister? You're not meeting with this person."

"I'm going to call him, Ryan. This is how I get a lot of my leads."

"A lot of your leads end up putting you in harm's way."

She worked the crumpled paper from his fist and smoothed it out on her knee. "It's a phone number. It can't hurt to call."

"Let's take this upstairs."

Ryan kept a firm hand on her back as they went up to her room, as if he could protect her that way from the person who'd written her the note.

Who *had* written the note? Could it have been Rebecca Leeds, having had a change of heart? No, they'd just left her place. Marie Giardano?

As soon as her room door closed, she reached for her cell phone.

"Wait." Ryan put out a hand. "Call on Speaker. And there's no way you're meeting this person alone, if that's what he's asking. And we're calling the police this time."

"Okay, okay." She would have agreed to any of his terms at that point. They needed some fresh information, a fresh point of view.

With shaky fingers, she tapped in the number from the note.

A gruff voice answered after the first ring. "Kacie?"

Her heart skipped a beat. Did he have her phone number, too? "Yes. How'd you know that?"

"You're the only one who has this number, Kacie. Do you want the truth? You and Brody?"

Her gaze shifted to Ryan's narrowed eyes. "Yes, of course. You mean the truth about Joey Brody and the real Phone Book Killer, right?"

"That's right, sweetheart."

She hunched her shoulders. "What is it? What is the truth? Tell me now."

He laughed and coughed at the same time. "It ain't that simple. I want to meet you."

Ryan shook his head back and forth so vigorously a lock of dark hair fell over his eye.

"I'll meet you, but you have to satisfy some conditions."

"I'm the one with the 411. Why are you calling the shots? You remind me of someone."

"Let me guess—your sister?"

"I ain't got no sister."

"Good. I'm not meeting you alone."

"Bring Brody with you. Is that what you want? He deserves the truth, too."

Ryan's jaw tensed and a muscle jumped in his throat.

"I will bring him. When and where?"

"No time like the present. Meet me down at the wharf at eleven tonight."

"I met someone else at the wharf earlier this week. It didn't end so well."

"Duke? He was an amateur."

"You knew him?"

"I know his kind. In over his head."

"And you're not?"

"I never spent a day in prison, sweetheart."

"Congratulations. Where are we meeting on the wharf? At the busy end. Someplace public."

"No. What I have to say to you and Brody is private. I'm lettin' you bring your big, strong man with you. That should be good enough. And do I have to tell you no cops? Calling the cops will only hurt you."

Her eyes met Ryan's and she shrugged. "I don't know."

"Are you telling me Brody's too scared to meet with me?"

"I'm not too scared to meet with you, but if you so much as touch Kacie, you're a dead man."

"I believe you, Brody." He hacked out a cough again. "Eleven o'clock by the submarine. There's a nice view of the bridge from there."

He hung up before Ryan could respond.

Kacie cupped the phone in her hand. "It sounds promising, doesn't it?"

"Why? Just because some guy calls out of the blue, seems to know what you're working on and tells you he has information? This could be anyone, Kacie. I don't like it."

"Of course you don't like it, but it's the way I work."

"And this is the way *I* work." He punched a number into his own phone and said, "I need to speak to Detective John Curtis or Lieutenant Healy."

As he paused, she grabbed his arm. "He said no cops."

He held his hand over the receiver. "The cops are not going to stake out a meeting between an author and a source. I just want them to be aware of what's going down."

He got Curtis on the phone and told him about the anonymous phone call. "Yeah, I have my weapon, and I'll keep you posted."

"What are they going to do?"

"Nothing for now, but they might send a patrol car over if one's in the area. Maybe they'll just sit there as reinforcement in case he tries something."

"I have a good feeling about this, Ryan. I heard something in his voice."

"Yeah, cigarettes and hard living. Sounded a lot like Duke Bannister."

"With one major difference."

"He doesn't have a sister?"

"He's never been to prison."

The rest of the evening dragged by, and although Ryan managed to scarf down a big meal from room service, she barely touched her pasta.

She had instincts and she had a feeling about this one.

When the digital clock ticked over to 10:30, she put on a pair of running shoes and yanked a hooded sweatshirt from the hook by the door. "I'm ready."

"We're about a ten-minute walk from the sub. Relax."

"Impossible." She bounced on the edge of the bed.

Ryan knelt in front of her, placing his hands on her knees. "I need to get back to Crestview in a few days. When I go, I want you to leave this alone."

Her breath caught in her throat. She'd almost forgotten he had a job to get back to. She'd almost forgotten he had another life beyond this city, beyond this hotel, beyond this case.

"I can't leave it alone, Ryan." She curled her hands around his biceps. "I'm writing this book."

"When you started writing the book, you had no idea it would lead to dead bodies, disappearances and your own kidnapping. It's a good thing I was here through all of that, but I can't be here forever."

"You mean you can't be with me forever."

"I didn't mean that." He put his hands around her waist. "I can't say what's going to happen between us, but if anything does, it's going to have to be away from all this. It's the only way to tell if it's for real."

"I know what's real, Ryan Brody. My feelings for you are real." She rested her cheek on top of his hair. "Are you telling me there can be no us as long as I'm working on this book?"

"I don't know, Kacie." He kissed her and whispered in her ear. "It's time to go."

They walked to the wharf hand in hand. Was he right? Did the feelings they had for each other now exist in some alternate reality where fear and danger fueled their attraction? Would they have to step away from the fire to see the truth?

They crossed the street to the wharf and turned left, toward the submarine. A cop car crawled down the street and Kacie poked Ryan in the ribs. "Do you think that's our backup?"

"Possibly." He patted his jacket pocket. "I've got our first line of defense right here."

"I'm hoping it won't come to that. He'll give us the info we've been waiting for and slither back under his rock."

"Don't count on it." He squeezed her hand, but it didn't soften his words.

Their steps slowed as they approached the closed ticket counter for the submarine. Ryan turned his back to the counter, his posture erect and alert.

A man climbed the steps to the walkway. "You made it."

"We're here. Now, what do you have for us?" Kacie took a step forward at the same time the man stepped under the circle of light from the lamp hanging above his head.

"Stop." Ryan grabbed her arm and yanked her back. "Don't you recognize him, Kacie? He's the man who tried to abduct you."

Kacie stumbled back against Ryan's chest as she squinted across the darkness—same height, same prominent nose, same gray hair.

Her heart pounded. "It's you, isn't it?"

"Guilty as charged." The man spread his arms wide. "But I can explain."

Ryan drew his gun from his pocket and released the safety with a click. "You'd better start explaining right now."

"I just wanted to talk to you, Kacie."

"And *that's* the method you chose? Drugging me? Carrying me off in my pajamas?"

"It seemed like a good plan at the time. I had a car waiting by the side of the hotel. I was just going to whisk you away for a private meeting, a little one-on-one time."

"Why? Why all this scheming?"

"I figured if I told you the truth, you'd never agree to meet me."

"That you had information for me? Why wouldn't I agree to meet you?"

"It's more than that, sweetheart."

"Stop calling me that."

"What's the truth? Let's hear it." Ryan had taken a step forward, shielding her body with his.

"The truth? I'm your father, Kacie. I'm Russ Langford. Layla French was my girl. She had my daughter on February fourteenth—Kacie Louise. 'Louise' after my mother."

Her body stiffened as the truth of his words hit her. "Why now? Why are you contacting me now and what do you have to do with the Brody case?"

"The Brody case is *my* case."

Ryan waved his gun. "What the hell are you talking about?"

"Kacie, I'm your father and I'm the Phone Book Killer."

Chapter Fifteen

His words roared in her ears and seemed to echo up and down the wharf. Then she laughed, a high-pitched giggle that frightened her as much as his proclamation had.

Ryan wound his arm around her waist as if to hold her up.

He growled at the man. "What are you talking about? Your ex was one of the Phone Book Killer's victims."

"The first and the only one who mattered."

"Wh-what are you saying? You killed my mother?"

"She'd left me and had taken you with her."

"You abused her."

Ryan's arm tightened around Kacie's waist.

"That's what they called it, but what we had was explosive." He shrugged. "We lost control sometimes."

"*You* lost control."

"Wait a minute." Ryan squared his shoulders. "Are you saying you killed Layla French, and then someone else killed the others, and because the M.O. was the same, Layla's murder was tied to the others?"

"No, Brody. I'm saying I was the Phone Book Killer. I killed Layla, and then I killed the others to cover the motive. After Layla's murder, the cops were trying to find me in Ohio. I killed the others to get them off my trail."

"You killed other people just to cover one crime?" Her stomach flipped and she felt like vomiting.

"It's not like I hadn't done it before. There were a few people in Ohio I had to get rid of."

Kacie gagged and covered her mouth.

"That's one of the reasons Layla left me. She had her suspicions."

Ryan snorted. "So all that bull about true love is just that. You came after Layla because you were afraid she'd rat you out."

"There was that."

"And the notes to my father? The kidnapping of my brother? Why did you go through all that?"

He pushed his hands forward. "I didn't."

"Liar. The Phone Book Killer contacted my father when he started investigating the second murder."

"It wasn't me. I told you. I've never been to prison, and that's why. I always kept a low profile. I'd never contact a cop like that."

"You're saying some random person started sending those notes? And what about the kidnapping?"

"I never touched your brother. Why would I do that?"

"Oh, I don't know. You're a cold-blooded killer."

Kacie was leaning so heavily against him he was afraid she was going to fall over. Her body had started trembling and shaking.

"Believe me or not, Brody. I had nothing to do with your brother's kidnapping or those notes to your father."

"I don't believe you, Langford. Why are you coming forward now after all these years?"

He shifted from one foot to the other. "Because my daughter's writing a book, and I want to give her a story. I owe her that."

"You owe me that? You owe me my mother."

"You know, sweetheart, you ended up better off. That

nice family adopted you and moved you up to Seattle. Your mother was a whore."

Kacie's trembling stopped and her muscles tensed.

"Shut the hell up, Langford. You murdered your daughter's mother and you think she needs a story? What are you really after?"

"Okay, you got me. I also happen to be dying—lung cancer. What do I have to lose now?"

"Then you can end your miserable life by telling the whole truth. What happened to my father?"

"He killed himself, as far as I know. Once that happened, I figured it was a good time to leave the city."

"And Bannister? You killed him because he was going to tell Kacie the truth?"

"I never touched Bannister."

"You beat up Cookie for the same reason?"

"I don't know any Cookie."

"Just stop lying." Kacie took a step toward her father, but Ryan held on to her arm. "You're dying. Just stop with the lies, unless that's a lie, too."

He coughed as if to prove the veracity of his claim. "Why would I lie now? Everything I told you tonight is the truth. I killed your mother because she left me. She wasn't my first kill, and she wasn't my last. I tried to disguise my motive by killing others in the same way, and I did pick them out of the phone book, within reason. I did not send any notes to Detective Brody, I did not kidnap his son, and the only thing I've done since I've been back in this city is try to get close to you, sweetheart."

"Don't. Call. Me. Sweetheart."

Langford chuckled. "Feisty, just like your mother. But that feistiness got her in trouble. So watch yourself, sweetheart."

Kacie wrenched away from Ryan and flew at her father.

"Kacie, stop!"

Before Ryan could reach them, Langford had his arm around Kacie's neck and a gun to her head.

He raised his own weapon. "Let her go. This isn't what you came here for."

"It's not, but I won't put up with this stuff from any woman. And you wonder why I drugged you in the first place? I wanted to have control when I made my confession to guard against something like this."

"Now you've made your confession. Let her go and be on your way."

Langford tightened his hold on Kacie. "You're not going to write any of this until I'm gone, right?"

She coughed and gagged.

"She can't breathe. Let her go. Even if she does write your story, she can't prove any of it."

"I don't need the cops investigating me before I kick the bucket."

Kacie gasped. "I'm not writing this story. Let me go and disappear. I never want to see you again."

"I don't know. Maybe this wasn't such a good idea. I thought you'd be grateful. Instead you're just like your mother, just like Layla."

He wrapped his arm tighter around Kacie's neck and she kicked his shin. He staggered back and the hand with the weapon dropped.

Kacie twisted away from him, and Ryan charged. He knocked the older man backward.

Langford still had his weapon, and he swung it toward Kacie. Ryan rolled between them and tensed his body, ready for the bullet meant for Kacie.

The shot rang out and Langford grunted. Had he missed?

"Kacie?"

"I'm okay."

Another shot echoed along the wharf and Ryan twisted his body to get a look at Langford.

He had flung his arms out to the side, his gun inches from his hand, a pool of blood spreading along the pavement beneath his head.

"Is everyone all right?" A bright light flooded the area, and two uniformed cops rushed forward, brandishing their service revolvers.

Ryan squinted at them as he pulled Kacie into his arms. "Did you shoot him?"

"No, sir. We had a sniper set up. When he grabbed Ms. Manning and put a gun to her head, the sniper got to work."

A million questions assaulted his brain, but Kacie needed him. Deep sobs racked her body and he sat up against the chain-link fence, pulling her into his lap.

"It's okay now. It's okay. It's all over."

She raised her tear-streaked face. "It's not over. It's just beginning."

"No, no, Kacie. You're fine. It's going to be okay."

"It's not okay, Ryan."

"It's hard. I know it's hard, but we'll get through it together."

"All this time, I thought your father was the killer and he wasn't. It was mine. My father was the killer."

Epilogue

Kacie zipped up her suitcase and scanned the hotel room once more. "Do you think I should even leave a tip after everything I went through here?"

"Hey, it wasn't the maids' fault." Ryan pulled back the drapes, and sunlight filtered into the room.

She reached into her wallet and pulled out a twenty. "It's tax-deductible anyway."

"Are you going to be doing any writing in Crestview?"

She sat next to one of her bags on the bed and pinned her hands between her knees. "I don't know, Ryan. I need time to process all this. How do you deal with it? How do you come to terms with the fact that your father is responsible for taking human lives and causing such destruction and despair?"

"Why don't you talk to someone, Kacie? I know a great therapist in town. We work with her all the time."

"It's ironic, isn't it? All those years I blamed Joseph Brody for my mother's death, and it turned out to have been my own father."

"We'll see about that. When that DNA test comes back, it may turn out Langford was lying anyway. I don't know how much to believe about what he said."

Ryan insisted on giving her hope by suggesting that

Russ Langford wasn't really her father, but she'd rather not harbor that wish.

She tucked her hair behind one ear. "Why would he lie about being the Phone Book Killer? He never wanted the publicity for the crimes."

"That part makes sense, but what about all that other stuff? What about Bannister, the doll, Cookie, the initial attack on you in the steam room and someone trying to get to your computer? Even the brakes on my car. He denied all involvement." Ryan crossed his arms and wedged his shoulder against the window.

"I was thinking about that. Maybe the steam room, the doll and Bannister were all Walker's doing, his way of punishing me."

"What about Cookie? Walker had nothing to do with her beating, and we can't ask her because she's still in a coma."

"Did you ever think that what happened to Cookie was unrelated to everything else? Someone attacked her at an open house. Maybe someone from her past."

"And Marie's disappearance?"

"You said it yourself. She was paranoid." She clapped her hands together. "Maybe now that Russ Langford's confession is out there, she'll feel safe enough to come home. I already told Ray Lopez he's welcome to the Langford story."

"Is he picking it up?"

"I don't know. Without the Brody connection, he didn't seem quite as interested. He believes Langford was the Phone Book Killer, but he's still intrigued by the unanswered questions surrounding the case."

"For once, Lopez is right." Ryan scratched his chin and sat beside her on the bed. It dipped and she shifted against his solid shoulder.

"There's so much that doesn't make sense," he said,

"and we're still left with the greatest mystery of all. Why did my father jump from the Golden Gate Bridge?"

"A lot of people wonder that about their friends and relatives. None of us knows what drives other people. Your father could've suffered from depression. The case might have been the last straw."

"I don't know if I can ever accept that, Kacie."

"I know. There's a lot I can't accept." She took his hand. "But I can't deal with it right now, Ryan. I'm putting the book aside. I feel like I granted my mom a measure of justice."

"I think you did." He slipped an arm around her shoulders. "I'm sorry to keep harping on it. You need a break. Hell, I need a break."

"*She* needs a break." She pointed at the TV, where a horde of reporters was following London Breck out of the courthouse, yelling questions at her. The blonde in the large sunglasses didn't answer one of them, instead ducking into a waiting limo.

"I told you. Sometimes money is a curse." He squeezed her shoulder. "Let's get out of this city."

"You love this city. We both do."

"Yeah, but what did Cookie say? Sometimes it just gets to be too much."

Kacie turned and put her arms around his neck. "We have a chance, don't we, Ryan? I just want to start over with you, away from the drama and the danger and the lies. My lies."

He kissed her and she knew everything was going to be okay.

After he took her breath away, he traced her lips with his finger. "I'm going to take care of you in Crestview, and you can write whatever you want to write. There's a big mystery going on right now about who's stealing Mr.

Pritchard's tomatoes. The book could be explosive. Another bestseller."

Smiling, she rested her head against his chest. They could start over. She had found love—with one of the sons of Joseph Brody.

* * * * *

*Don't miss the heart-stopping conclusion of
BRODY LAW when Carol Ericson's THE HILL
goes on sale next month. Look for it wherever
Harlequin Intrigue books are sold!*

REQUEST YOUR FREE BOOKS!
2 FREE NOVELS PLUS 2 FREE GIFTS!

HARLEQUIN

INTRIGUE

BREATHTAKING ROMANTIC SUSPENSE

YES! Please send me 2 FREE Harlequin Intrigue® novels and my 2 FREE gifts (gifts are worth about $10). After receiving them, if I don't wish to receive any more books, I can return the shipping statement marked "cancel." If I don't cancel, I will receive 6 brand-new novels every month and be billed just $4.74 per book in the U.S. or $5.24 per book in Canada. That's a savings of at least 14% off the cover price! It's quite a bargain! Shipping and handling is just 50¢ per book in the U.S. and 75¢ per book in Canada.* I understand that accepting the 2 free books and gifts places me under no obligation to buy anything. I can always return a shipment and cancel at any time. Even if I never buy another book, the two free books and gifts are mine to keep forever.

182/382 HDN F42N

Name	(PLEASE PRINT)

Address		Apt. #

City	State/Prov.	Zip/Postal Code

Signature (if under 18, a parent or guardian must sign)

Mail to the **Harlequin® Reader Service:**
IN U.S.A.: P.O. Box 1867, Buffalo, NY 14240-1867
IN CANADA: P.O. Box 609, Fort Erie, Ontario L2A 5X3

**Are you a subscriber to Harlequin Intrigue books
and want to receive the larger-print edition?
Call 1-800-873-8635 or visit www.ReaderService.com.**

* Terms and prices subject to change without notice. Prices do not include applicable taxes. Sales tax applicable in N.Y. Canadian residents will be charged applicable taxes. Offer not valid in Quebec. This offer is limited to one order per household. Not valid for current subscribers to Harlequin Intrigue books. All orders subject to credit approval. Credit or debit balances in a customer's account(s) may be offset by any other outstanding balance owed by or to the customer. Please allow 4 to 6 weeks for delivery. Offer available while quantities last.

Your Privacy—The Harlequin® Reader Service is committed to protecting your privacy. Our Privacy Policy is available online at www.ReaderService.com or upon request from the Harlequin Reader Service.

We make a portion of our mailing list available to reputable third parties that offer products we believe may interest you. If you prefer that we not exchange your name with third parties, or if you wish to clarify or modify your communication preferences, please visit us at www.ReaderService.com/consumerschoice or write to us at Harlequin Reader Service Preference Service, P.O. Box 9062, Buffalo, NY 14269. Include your complete name and address.

HI13R

SPECIAL EXCERPT FROM

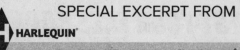
HARLEQUIN®

I N T R I G U E ®

When a woman from his past shows up with newborn twins and claims she needs his protection, a Texas lawman will risk everything to keep them all safe…

Read on for an excerpt from
COWBOY BEHIND THE BADGE
by USA TODAY *bestselling author*

Delores Fossen

Laine didn't push him away. A big surprise. But she did look up at him. "Ironic, huh? When you woke up yesterday morning, I'll bet you never thought we'd be voluntarily touching each other."

Tucker shook his head, hoping it'd clear it. It didn't work. Maybe he should try hitting it against the wall. "Who says this is voluntary?"

A short burst of air left her mouth. Almost a laugh. Then that troubled look returned to her eyes. "It's not a good idea for us to be here alone."

"No. It's not."

There. They were in complete agreement. Still, neither of them moved a muscle. Well, he moved some. His grip tightened on her a little, and those kissing dreams returned with a vengeance.

"Besides, I'm no longer your type," she added, as if that would help.

It didn't.

However, it did cause him to temporarily scowl. "How

would you know my type?"

Another huff. Soft and silky, though, not rough like his. Her breath brushed against his mouth almost like a kiss. Almost. "Everyone in town knows. Blonde, busty and not looking for a commitment."

He was sure his scowl wasn't so brief that time, but the problem was he couldn't argue with her about it. Besides, the reminder accomplished what Laine had likely intended.

Tucker stepped back from her.

He figured that she'd say something smart-mouthed to keep things light, but she didn't. For a moment Laine actually looked a little disappointed that their little hugging session had ended, and that was all the more reason for him to not pick it up again.

Ever.

Even if parts of him were suggesting just that.

With killers hot on their trail and innocent babies in need of protection, a sizzling attraction should be the last thing on Tucker's and Laine's minds.

Find out how long they'll be able to contain it when the second book in USA TODAY *bestselling author Delores Fossen's* **SWEETWATER RANCH** *miniseries,* COWBOY BEHIND THE BADGE, *goes on sale in October 2014!*

INTRIGUE

**THE PAST HAUNTS TWO DETERMINED
PEOPLE LOOKING FOR ANSWERS IN
PAULA GRAVES'S NEXT INSTALLMENT
OF *THE GATES*.**

For twenty years, Cain Dennison has been haunted by
the death of a young pregnant girl found murdered at
Crybaby Falls. Determined to finally discover the truth
and lay the past to rest, Cain quickly discovers he's
not the only one looking for answers. Crossing paths
with Sara Lindsey at the very spot that has caused
so much pain, Cain is stunned to discover an instant
and dangerous attraction flaring between them. Their
shared goal of finding answers only fuels their passion—
and enrages a killer. Before long, they stumble across
information that could affect everyone in this small
Tennessee town…and bring the real culprit right
to their doorstep.

CRYBABY FALLS

BY PAULA GRAVES

*Only from Harlequin® Intrigue®.
Available October 2014 wherever
books and ebooks are sold.*

INTRIGUE

AS A P.I., HE WAS USED TO PROTECTING PEOPLE. BUT ONE BEAUTIFUL HEIRESS IS CHALLENGING EVERY MOVE HE MAKES IN THE CONCLUSION OF CAROL ERICSON'S *BRODY LAW* MINISERIES.

When P.I. Judd Brody agreed to safeguard socialite London Breck, he expected a fluff gig filled with parties and paparazzi. But the bombshell blonde was nothing like the wild princess he'd seen in the media…and his undeniable attraction to her was as real as the threats to her life.

The missteps of London's past didn't compare to the fear she now faced. With her sexy bodyguard by her side, she vowed to confront the conspiracy haunting her family. London couldn't imagine surviving this without Judd. She'd help him get the answers she needed. But she had no intention of watching him walk away once he did….

THE HILL

BY CAROL ERICSON

Only from Harlequin® Intrigue®.
Available October 2014 wherever
books and ebooks are sold.

INTRIGUE

A HOLIDAY RESCUE AT
THUNDER HORSE RANCH

En route to investigate an illegal crossing, border patrol
agent Dante Thunder Horse's helicopter goes down
in a fiery blaze. He makes it out of the wreckage—
just barely—and tackles his assailant to the ground.
Paleontologist Emma Jennings is no killer—but she's now
in the crosshairs of one. Sworn to protect the woman
who saved him, Dante needs to find out who shot
him down and why.

When Emma accompanies Dante back to his Badlands
ranch, where a vengeful enemy threatens his family
and their proud heritage, she's in even more danger...
of falling for the brave Lakota pilot. But can there be a
future with a man haunted by the past?

CHRISTMAS AT THUNDER
HORSE RANCH
BY ELLE JAMES

*Only from Harlequin® Intrigue®.
Available October 2014 wherever
books and ebooks are sold.*

HI69792